To: Oliver

ENJOY THE ADVENTURE!!

SONIA

Annabellia

An Adventure for the Ages

Sean O'Neill

Copyright © 2021 Sean O'Neill
All rights reserved
First Edition

Fulton Books, Inc.
Meadville, PA

Published by Fulton Books 2021

ISBN 978-1-64952-809-4 (paperback)
ISBN 978-1-64952-811-7 (hardcover)
ISBN 978-1-64952-810-0 (digital)

Printed in the United States of America

ACKNOWLEDGEMENTS

A book may only have one author, but I find it hard to believe that any author can accomplish his or her goal without the help and support of others. I have several people that I need to thank for helping me achieve this accomplishment. First and foremost, I would like to thank my incredible wife Diane who is always there to support me. Regardless of whatever crazy endeavor I decide to take on, I can always count on her to stand behind me. I am also grateful for the strength and prideful support provided by my children, Courtney, Gabrielle, Hugh and Lauren. My parents Tom and Bernardine also deserve kudos. They are responsible, along with my five siblings, for the imagination, creativity, and humor that I have developed over my lifetime. In addition, just like her daughter, my mother-in-law, Joanne Lee, has shown me nothing but unconditional support. I would also like to send a special shout out to all the guys at the fire station; they seem as excited about this book as I am. Also, a big thanks to fellow firefighter David Soriano for the tremendous cover and illustrations. Finally, I could not have done this without Peter Harvan. Peter spent countless hours on this project, helping me turn an idea into a novel!

Chapter 1

I watched the ball soar about fifty feet over my head. Johnny "Haas" Johnson had just blasted a baseball farther than I had ever seen someone hit one in my life, and for the record, I was a die-hard Yankees fan. Okay, so I grew up near Cleveland but cheered for the Yankees. So what? So did LeBron! Anyway, I turned and followed the ball with my eyes. I didn't even take a step as it cleared the ten-foot-high bushes and disappeared into the creek below. Our local baseball diamond didn't have a fence. It was in a large pasture with nothing but grass in both right and center fields. The only thing that could be called a home run fence were the bushes in left field, and coincidentally, that was also the only place you could lose a ball. I stood with my mouth wide open, looking at the bushes and trying to comprehend how far that ball had just traveled. I was in awe.

"Get the ball, you butthead!" my older brother Michael screamed at me as he wandered from the shortstop position into left field.

"Okay, Francis!" I yelled back. Francis was my brother's middle name, and he loathed it. Whenever I wanted to get under his skin, well, that was my go-to card. He hated it even more when I used his middle name in front of his friends. I turned and started jogging toward the creek with a big satisfied smile on my face, chuckling as I heard his friends taunting him and calling him Francis.

It was an unseasonably warm October day in Ohio, and my brother and his friends had invited me to play baseball with them. Michael said it was because it was my birthday, but I knew that they had already called everyone else in their address books and they still needed one more to make the teams even. I didn't feel the need to let Michael know that I was wise to him. I was just happy to be playing. It was my tenth birthday, and not only was I playing with a bunch of eleven-, twelve-, and thirteen-year-olds but I was better than a couple of them. I was feeling pretty good about myself.

I climbed down the steep creek wall to the rocks below. The water was lower than normal because not only was it warmer than usual, it hadn't rained in a couple of weeks. I brushed the sandy brown hair from my blue eyes and quickly located the ball in an inch or two of water about twenty feet upstream. I made my way to it, attempting to keep my birthday sneakers dry.

I reached for the ball, but when I picked it up, a sparkling burst of light with every color imaginable came shooting up through the ground. The light continued to glow on the dirty clay bank of the creek bed about two feet from where the ball was sitting. It was hard to look at because it was so bright. My head was half turned. My face was scrunched up. My right eye was completely closed, and my left eye barely opened while I tried to figure out what I was looking at.

Suddenly, *poof!* With a small puff of white smoke, the light was gone. When the smoke dissipated, there appeared a little bright-green frog. I mean really bright—sparkly even. Oddly enough, the frog had a pointy white beard, and he was also wearing a wizard hat. He was standing on his two hind legs; and he was holding, well, more like leaning on, what appeared to be a cane or a long magic wand. The walking stick was black with a white tip that was resting on the ground.

Speechless and in shock, I stared at the sight. Now, I was facing this, well, amphibian with both my eyes, as well as my mouth wide open.

"Close your mouth, Daniel," the frog said. "It's rude, and I don't need to see how many cavities you have." He paused and looked at me. "Just for the record, it's five."

"Huh?" was all I could muster.

"Five cavities. You should really brush before bed. I bet you just wet your toothbrush in order to fool your folks."

He was correct, but that didn't seem to register right away or even matter to me. "Who...what..." I shook my head back and forth rapidly with my eyes closed.

I opened them up, and as soon as I did, the frog started doing a little dance. He was now holding his wand in both hands, shaking his hips, and moving the wand forward and backward. He then slammed the white tip on the ground with his right hand and spun around. "Ta-da!" he exclaimed as he leaned toward me, bent at the knees with a big smile on his face.

To make things even more awkward, his smile consisted of what looked to be perfectly straight bright-white teeth. Do frogs even have teeth?

"I'm still here," he said with a little laugh.

I dropped the ball and sat down on a nearby rock and just stared at this...frog, my mouth still agape. The frog leaned in toward me with his eyes wide open and kind of nodded his head a couple of times as if he was inviting me to ask a question.

"Okay, okay, I'll start," he finally said. "You are actually doing much better than the last two kids I encountered. They both ran away screaming. The kid before those two actually tried to smash me with a rock. Before that was a girl. She didn't seem scared at all. And she talked with me for quite a while before she left to go home, which brings me to the boy before her. He is from your neighborhood. Do you know Tommy—"

"Tommy Anderson," I said rather quietly, cutting him off before he could finish the name. Tommy lived down the street from me, and he had been missing for about a month. He was a year younger than I was. We didn't hang out together. It was not that I disliked him, but we didn't have a whole lot in common. Tommy had an older brother named Darryl who was sixteen and a bit of a troublemaker. He also had an older sister, Courtney, who was fourteen and liked the bad boys. And her boyfriend, Caleb, was the epitome of a bad boy. All signs indicated that Tommy was going to follow in the family's footsteps.

"Yes, Tommy Anderson," the frog stated. "He needs help, and right now you are the only one who is able to come with me to provide it."

Before I could respond, I heard one of the older kids yell from the ball diamond. "Hurry up, Danny! Danny, Danny who wears his mommy's panties." This was then followed by loud laughter from all the others.

I ignored the call and asked the frog, "Why me?" Oh my god, was I really indulging in a conversation with this… this… "What are you?" I blurted out.

"A forg" was the reply.

"A frog?" I asked.

"No, a forg. I am like a frog. Well, I guess I'm like a frog. But I'm magic," he said with some showmanship as a puff of smoke came from his fingers. "Your friends will be coming soon. We have to go now," the forg stated with a little urgency, as well as authority, in his voice.

"Where?" was my answer.

"To the magical kingdom of Annabellia."

"Why would I go with you?" I asked, sounding a bit perturbed.

"Because only the special ones can, and they only have one opportunity to open the gateway between our worlds." I looked at him, and I was actually entertaining his explanation. He continued, "You see, Tommy came to our world on September 9." I thought for a second, and that date sounded like the date that Tommy disappeared. "It was his birthday," the forg stated. I was quite sure that was accurate because that was all anyone had talked about. "He just turned nine." Again, I agreed with the little green creature. "Do you see the similarity between him and you, Daniel?" I shook my head no. "Tommy turned nine on September 9…9-9-9. You turn ten today, October 10…10-10-10. This is the only way the gateway opens. Tommy came to us on September 9, and well, he got into some trouble. Most of the people in my world are kind and treat humans like royalty. Tommy, however, trusted the wrong people, and now he is in danger of never coming home. You need to help him."

I heard voices approaching as my brother and a couple others were getting close to the creek. "If they see me, I will disappear forever, and you will lose your chance to come to Annabellia and help Tommy," whispered the forg.

"Why me? Why can't you wave your magic wand and help him get home?" I pleaded.

"You see, Daniel, like I possess magic in your world, you possess magic in ours. I am completely normal back home. But you, Daniel, you can accomplish beautiful, wonderful things there. You won't regret coming with me, and only you can help Tommy get home." I heard rustling in the bushes and some indistinct chatter coming from my brother's mouth. "Quick, grab my wand and we will go. Otherwise, this opportunity will be lost forever."

Now I have always been brave. My mom would even call me a little reckless. I had to be. I was ten, and I was small. But I would still play tackle football with the older kids. I was tough for my size, and I could hold my own. I also had a weakness: curiosity. Curiosity had landed me in hot water more than a couple of times. But the forg said I would possess magic and do incredible things. This was pretty hard to resist.

I heard my brother's voice. "Daniel? Where the heck are you?"

I grabbed the wand.

Chapter 2

With one bright-white flash, I was standing in a new world. The land was beautiful and intensely green—greener than Ireland. There were trees and colorful birds that were singing and flitting around everywhere. Off in the distance, I saw a wonderful waterfall that must've been two hundred feet high. It was splashing down into a bright-blue pool of water. The sky was clear, and the air was fresh.

I stood there in awe while turning in a slow circle, trying to absorb the beauty that surrounded me when all of the sudden…"Well, what do you think?"

I looked down and saw a little white-haired man with a fluffy beard down to his belly. I jumped back, startled. I examined the man from head to toe. He wore a white shirt with blue suspenders, blue pants, and shiny black shoes with gold buckles. Even though he had white hair, he wasn't an old man. He had smooth pale skin and rosy cheeks. He was short—I mean really short. I was only ten years old and far from big for my age, but I had to be a foot taller than this guy. He was wearing a pointed blue witch-like hat that matched his pants and suspenders, and the hat had a gold capital *M* in the middle. I'm not trying to be offensive, but he reminded me of the gnomes from my dad's garden.

"Excuse me," I said. "Who…who are you?"

"The name's Mitchell." The voice sounded familiar, but I had certainly never seen this man before.

I was so confused. Everything was happening so fast. "Where's the forg?" I was able to muster up.

"Ha ha!" Mitchell belted out. "There's no such thing as a forg! Don't you know a frog when you see one?" I cocked my head and stared into his eyes.

"It's you! You're the forg!" I exclaimed, finally recognizing his voice.

Mitchell took a bow and said, "It is I...the frog!" Mitchell emphasized the word *frog*. "I told you there is no such thing as a forg. I just like messing with you kids when I come into your world," he continued. "You see, I am not always a frog when I come to your realm. I can be any animal I want. I chose to be a frog because they are not threatening, and well...you were in a stream. I couldn't have exactly been a talking camel in a creek in Ohio, now could I?" Even though I had a confused look on my face, I gave him an understanding nod of agreement. "Remember when I told you about the two kids who ran away screaming?" I nodded my head yes. "Well, once I was a mouse, and the other time I was a bee. Kid that tried to smash me... spider. I won't make those mistakes again. Oh, and the girl that talked to me for a while?" I nodded again. "Bunny rabbit. Who could resist a bunny rabbit, am I right?"

I felt as if Mitchell would never stop talking if I didn't say something. "Where am I? Why am I here, and how do I get home?" I felt those were all more than fair questions.

"You are in the wonderful world of Annabellia. Follow me, Daniel." It was an order, but he said it in a friendly way.

He waved his arm in a "come along" fashion. "We will discuss everything over some tea, or do you prefer coffee or cocoa?"

A confused "cocoa" was my reply.

"Cocoa it is then," Mitchell said smiling. "My place is right over here." We walked toward a giant tree. The trunk had to be twenty feet around, and I was unable to see the top through the mass of branches and green leaves. As we came closer, I could make out an outline of a door about four feet high. Mitchell, still carrying his wand, inserted the white tip into a small hole just to the right of the door. As it swung open, he commanded, "C'mon in and watch your head."

I followed him, ducking through the doorway, and made my way into the tree.

Chapter 3

The room we entered was like a kitchen. It had a wooden table with two wooden benches on either side. The table was only about two and a half feet off the floor, and the benches looked like they could fit a gnome family of four. Along the back wall of the room was a small stove with four burners and a teapot on one of them. Next to the stove was a sink, and above it, a small window covered by yellow curtains with a blue flower design. In the corner of the right side of the room, a small black bird perched on a swing inside a wooden birdcage. The bird had a thin yellow beak that was disproportionately long for its size coupled with tiny orange feet. On the left side of the room, there was a spiral staircase. I couldn't see where it led since there seemed to be a covering over the hole where it ended. To the right of the table sat a single soft-looking armchair. It was kind of faded and had a worn-out, lived-in look to it. The chair was red with gold stripes, and the stripes on the armrests were almost non-existent because of the wear. Next to the chair was an end table holding an empty teacup. The only picture on the wall was a painting of a flowerpot filled with bright-yellow flowers that looked like daffodils.

"Sit down, Daniel," Mitchell said invitingly. "I need to fill you in on how things work in the wonderful world of Annabellia." I sat down at the table as Mitchell filled the teakettle with milk and placed it on the stove. "First of all, and most importantly, time is different here. One day in Annabellia is equal to one minute on earth. So if you were here for a week, you would only be gone from earth for seven minutes. Do you follow me?" Mitchell asked. I nodded. I'm far from a math whiz; but that seemed like a pretty easy equation, even for me. Mitchell stood up and added some chocolate to the milk on the stove. "Secondly," he said turning around to face me, "humans age while they are here. However, when they return home, they revert back to their human age. Understand?" It was easy to see that I did not. "Okay, try to follow me." Mitchell sat back down and looked me in the eyes. If you stayed in Annabellia for one year, you would be how old here?" Mitchell asked.

"Eleven" was my answer.

"Perfect," he responded. "Now if you stayed here for a year and went home, how old would you be on earth?"

"Eleven?" My voice went up an octave and cracked because it was obvious that I was not sure.

"No, Daniel, you would be 10 years old and 365 minutes, which basically comes out to 10 years and 6 hours."

The light went on. "So if I was to go home right now, my brother wouldn't even know that I had gone because I would have been away for only a couple of seconds."

"Precisely," Mitchell said excitedly.

"Good. I would like to go home right now, please."

"Hold on, Daniel. What about Tommy? He needs your help, and you could be his last hope."

"Why am I his last hope?"

"Because he has been missing since September 9, right?"

"Yes," I answered confusedly.

"That makes him about 131 years old! Now, humans can live a lot longer here than they can in your world, but nobody really knows exactly how long. Our best guess is that one of you could probably live until the age of around 150. We don't know for sure, and regardless, Tommy is becoming weaker by the day."

I stopped Mitchell right there. "So he's got…" I paused and did some quick math. "Nineteen more years. That means I'm not his last hope! I want to go home!"

Mitchell got very serious. He leaned across the table and stuck his face inches from mine. "Tommy is weak and sick, and he doesn't have much time. He was manipulated by the evil queen and served under her for years. When he tried to escape, he was caught and shackled in a dungeon. We have sources on the inside, but it will take another human to save him because in Annabellia, humans possess the magic."

"Why can't Tommy use his own magic?" I questioned Mitchell.

"Queen Kathelina is the most magical, powerful human to have ever entered into our kingdom. She was also the first human to enter, some say as many as one thousand years ago in earth's time. Somehow, she is still young and beautiful. Tommy's magic is powerless against hers. And right now, he doesn't even have his wand. The queen has taken it. Listen to me, Daniel. You live near Tommy, so you can bring him home with your wand through your gateway." Mitchell stood up. He filled a couple of mugs with the hot chocolate and came back to the table, setting one mug in front of me and keeping the other for himself.

"How dangerous will this be?" I asked with a clear sense of concern in my voice.

"It could be very dangerous," Mitchell answered without hesitation.

"Very dangerous?" My voice raised. Mitchell nodded. "Then I would like to go home. I don't even like Tommy. We aren't even friends! Take me back to the portal right now! I want to go home!" Now there was anger in my voice. It wasn't that I really didn't like Tommy. I didn't even know Tommy. I knew that his older brother scared me; but Tommy never did anything wrong, at least not that I could think of right now.

"It's not a portal. It's a gateway!" Mitchell countered angrily. He continued, "No human has ever died in our kingdom. If you don't help, Tommy may be the first. He will never see his family again, and they will never see him. To make things worse, some say that if a human dies in Annabellia, all the gateways will be closed forever. Daniel, will you please help us help Tommy?" Mitchell begged.

I thought for only a second. "Nope," I replied. There was a long silence as we stared intensely into each other's eyes. Finally, I had to look away. I stared at the ground and sheepishly muttered, "I just wanna go home."

There was a long pause. Mitchell broke the silence replying, "So be it, Daniel." I will take you back to the gateway. However, the gateway will remain open for you should you wish to return." We got up from the table and left the tree house through the still-open door. We silently returned to the exact spot where we had first arrived. The colorful birds were still flying around and singing, and I could see the beautiful waterfall in the distance.

Mitchell pointed to a tree about ten feet to my left. "There is a small hole in that tree trunk about three feet up from the ground." As he handed me a wand, he instructed, "Place the white tip of this wand in the hole and twist." I quickly snatched the wand, and when I did, it immediately sparkled and grew to about two feet in length.

"There is also a small hole in the rock near where you first saw me. Should you decide to come back, just stick the wand in that hole and twist, and you will find yourself back here." He looked down at the ground and rubbed the grass with his right foot.

I walked slowly to the tree, reached the wand toward the hole, and inserted the tip. "Daniel!" Mitchell interrupted, and I looked back at him. "Please remember that every minute you are gone is a full day here."

"Sure," I replied and twisted the wand.

Chapter 4

Just like that, I was back in the creek, and I was standing in a couple inches of water—the wand in my right hand and the ball on the ground a few feet away.

"The ball's getting soaked, you moron!" I heard one of the thirteen-year-olds yell. They must have just arrived at the creek because they obviously didn't see me reappear. I looked down at the ball and slowly bent over to pick it up. I grabbed it, stood back up, and silently held it out.

Haas snatched it and held it over his head. "Woo-hoo! Farthest home run ever!" He looked back and instantly exaggerated his accomplishment. "We have to be one hundred feet from the bushes!"

"What's with the wand, David Copperfield?" I heard someone ask. I didn't think he wanted an answer. He just felt like being a smart-ass. I studied the black stick with the white tip that I was holding. I lifted it up a tad, twisted it slowly, looked at it blankly, and without making eye contact with anyone, I shrugged my shoulders.

"C'mon, let's go," said another. "We got three more innings to play!"

Michael must have noticed the puzzled look on my face. "You okay, Daniel?" he asked. He actually sounded concerned.

My voice was barely more than a whisper when I answered him, still staring at the ground. "I have to go home," was my response.

"You can't!" The concern left his voice. "The game's not over yet."

"My shoes are wet," I mumbled. "I have to go home."

"You suck! This is the last time I'm gonna let you play with us!" In a huff, he started to climb the creek wall. He was the last one left as the others had run back to the field. I sat down. My butt was actually in the cold water a bit, but that didn't faze me at all.

Not moving, I sat there in the creek water. I was thinking about Tommy. I had barely said two words to that kid in my entire life. Why should he be my responsibility? Suddenly, I remembered a day last summer when I was walking by his house. I had just bought a brand-new basketball with the money I had been saving for weeks. I was dribbling the ball on the sidewalk when his older brother, Darryl, and one of his friends confronted me. Tommy was watching everything unfold from his front door. Darryl demanded that I give him my new ball as he stood in my way, blocking my path. I grabbed the ball with both hands and prepared for the worst. Just before things got real, Tommy flung the door open and shouted, "Darryl! Mom wants you!"

Darryl looked down at me and snarled, "You're lucky, punk." He turned and walked toward the house. I looked back to the door at Tommy. I was pretty sure he had just lied to save me from a beating. He dropped his eyes, turned, and disappeared inside.

Then I thought about what Mitchell said: "Remember that every minute you are gone is a whole day here." I looked down and saw the rock with the perfectly round hole just the size of the white tip of the wand. I inserted the stick, took a deep breath, and twisted it.

Chapter 5

With another bright-white flash, I was back in Annabellia, under the same beautiful tree with the beautiful birds and the beautiful waterfall tumbling in the distance. However, the worry and confusion that I now was feeling prevented me from appreciating what I was seeing. I looked to my left and saw Mitchell's house. I took a couple of steps toward it when his door flung open. Mitchell came walking briskly toward me with a giant smile on his face. "Oh, Daniel!" he exclaimed. "Thank you! Thank you! Thank you! I hoped you would come back! I knew you would come back! Well…I thought you would come back! Oh, I am so glad you're back! The king will be so excited!"

"The king?" I asked confusedly.

"Yes, the king! You didn't think little old Mitchell was in charge of everything, did you? But before you meet him, we need to discuss a few things. There are things that you need to be aware of. Powers that you possess and must control. Landmarks that will keep you safe. Friends to help and guide you and dangers to avoid. Now come back inside my house for your first lesson. You have so much to learn."

We walked back into the tree. "The classroom is upstairs," Mitchell stated. He led me to the spiral staircase, and up he went. I waited for him to get about halfway, and then I started my climb. He pushed open a door at the top and climbed through. The opening was kind of small, but I was able to enter the room without a problem. I crawled into the room on my knees then stood up and looked around. It appeared to be an old classroom. Four wooden desks were scattered around the room. Each desk held small piles of what looked like filler paper and a mug containing multiple pencils. In the front of the room, there was an old-style black chalkboard with chalk all along the shelf under it. To the right of the chalkboard hung a map with "Anabellia" written across the top.

"Sit," Mitchell said, pointing at the desk closest to the chalkboard, half ordering and half asking me to take a seat. "First thing's first. When do your parents expect you home?" Mitchell asked.

"I don't know," I answered.

"Okay." Slightly perturbed, Mitchell rephrased his question. "How long will it be before your parents start to wonder where you are and get worried?"

"I don't know. Maybe an hour," I said.

"Great!" Mitchell responded. "That gives us sixty days. We should have you home in plenty of time for your birthday dinner and cake." He clapped his hands, then closed and rubbed them together. "Now, let's get started." He looked at me and pointed to the wand. "Don't ever let that go. It will keep you safe, and it possesses great power. Now, anything that is vital to your very existence deserves a name. What do you want to name your wand?"

"My wand?" I said slowly. "Uhhh…"

"Wanda it is!" exclaimed Mitchell with satisfaction in his voice. He smiled, paused, and continued, "Daniel, you have a little sister at home, right?"

"Yes," I stated, "Molly."

"And you would do anything to protect Molly, correct?"

"Yes," I answered as I nodded.

"Great! Now you have a little sister here, and her name is Wanda. You need to know where she is at all times and protect her at all costs."

"Okay," I answered, a bit confused, thinking Mitchell was being a little dramatic.

"Great, now that we are clear on that, we will start simple." He paused, then finished his thought. "Hold it out in front of you."

"What?" I asked, confused.

His head slumped down, and he sighed. He looked back at me with disappointment. "Your wand!" he exclaimed with a little frustration in his voice. "Hold it out in front of you and get a feel for it." Wanda was about two feet in length. It wasn't the type of wand that you would see in the movies, but it looked like a version of a wand that you might find in a magic shop. It was more like a straight black cane with a few knots and a curved handle on top. Its surface felt like a combination of wood and plastic, but it didn't weigh much at all. It was shiny and smooth with a white tip on the bottom that was about an inch long. "The power is in the tip," Mitchell explained, never losing eye contact. "Point it at the chalkboard and flick your wrist."

I did as he said, and a little *zap* about the size of a spark of static electricity leaped from the end. It wasn't much, but it shocked me. "Whoa!" I said amazed.

"See," Mitchell said, "I told you that you would have power. Now put it in the wand holder on the side of your desk because it's time for a history lesson." He pointed to a wooden loop on the right side of my desk. I looked, and under the loop, there was a stack of six more loops about four inches apart. I slid Wanda in tip first until the white tip rested on the floor and the curved handle was hooked over the top loop. It wasn't a snug fit, but Wanda was secure. I looked to Mitchell for approval.

"I told you never to put your wand down!" Mitchell yelled dramatically. I fumbled trying to grab Wanda and lift her back out of the stacked loops. "Ha ha!" He chuckled. "Just bustin' your chops. You can put her in the holder, but outside this classroom, always, always, always have a hold of her." I put the wand back in the loops. He smiled, nodded, and said, "Where shall we begin?"

Chapter 6

"The king," Mitchell stated, "we shall start with the king." Using a stick with a little hook at the end, Mitchell reached up and pulled down on a metal ring hanging from a metal tube. It looked like one of those old maps that classrooms used to have, but when he unrolled it, there was a picture of a man on a throne. He was wearing a gold-and-purple coat with white fur around the collar. He had on white pants, black shoes, and a crown that looked like it was woven out of sticks. His skin was dark brown, and he had no hair—none at all. It seemed as if his head was shaved because it had a sheen to it. He was strikingly handsome, and even though he was wearing a thick coat, he was obviously fit and well-built. He wasn't smiling, but his serious expression couldn't hide his friendly appearance.

"King Salvatore is a great man!" Mitchell looked at me waiting for an acknowledgment. I nodded. "His family has ruled the kingdom of Annabellia for thousands of years. All the kings from this family have been generous and loving and have been wonderful protectors of all who live here, as well as those like you, Daniel, who come to visit our land. For centuries and centuries, young humans have entered our world, and every one of them has returned home safely. Some have come back to Annabellia throughout the years, and some we have never seen again. You see, once the gateway is opened, the special children with the special birthdays, like you, have the freedom to come and go as they please. The gateway remains accessible until your eighteenth earthen birthday. Breaking the wand is the only thing that can permanently close your gateway. However, one of the great kings of the past, King Fredrico, was able to make these wands virtually indestructible. They are fireproof, waterproof, and stronger than stone.

"The great kings of the past have ensured the safe passage of all visitors between our worlds. Usually the children come and have some fun for a few days or weeks and go home—no danger, no drama. And they are only gone for minutes from your world. Now, for the first time, we are faced with the possibility of not being able to send someone home."

"Tommy," I stated quietly, never losing eye contact with Mitchell.

"Yes," he answered, "Tommy Anderson is in grave danger of never going home, and King Salvatore has called on you for help." Mitchell turned and pointed to the map that I had noticed when I entered the room—a map of Annabellia. The map was mostly green but included rivers and mountains and a big lake labeled "Lake Montville." I also noticed yellow stars scattered throughout the map. "Every star that you see is a human gateway." Mitchell pointed to the bottom right corner of the map where there was a tiny tree with a star. "We are here, and here is your gateway," he stated with conviction. "The king lives here," he pointed to a castle labeled "Lordstown," which was just a tad below the center of the map. Mitchell continued, "And Tommy is here." Mitchell hit the map hard with his stick on the top left corner of the map where there was a black castle surrounded by gray. This gray area covered no more than 10 percent of the map. "This is the castle of Queen Kathelina. She is an evil person, Daniel. However, she has kept to herself in her corner of Annabellia for—" Mitchell looked at the ceiling "—well, for forever." Mitchell then pointed to a string of little black dots that circled the gray area on the map. "Over the last several years, though, she has been expanding her territory. King Salvatore has some spies under the queen's rule, and they have been reporting that she is raising and training a powerful army led by Princess Gabriella. There are rumors that they may attack the king's castle in the near future. We need to get to Tommy and bring him back to your gateway before any of this occurs."

I must have had a very frightened look on my face. "Don't worry, Daniel," Mitchell said sympathetically. "We will train you over the next several days to make sure that you are in control of your magic, and the king will devise a plan to minimize any dangers and risks that must be taken to rescue Tommy."

"Okay," I said softly and without 100 percent trust in my voice.

"It is my job to train you to use your wand and magic properly," Mitchell said with pride. "This usually takes about seven days or so. When I feel that you are ready, we will start the trek to meet the king." With his stick, Mitchell pointed to the small tree in the bottom right corner, and then dragged it to the castle near the middle of the map. "Our journey should take less than two days. This is a pretty safe area, and we should not encounter much danger. The only things we might need to worry about are the lolosters, but they are nocturnal. And we will pass their territory in daylight."

I didn't know what a loloster was, but I had a more important question on my mind. "What happened to Tommy?" I blurted out.

I must have caught him off guard and ruined his train of thought. He paused for a moment and looked up to the ceiling while he processed the question. "Tommy got careless and wandered off by himself. Princess Gabriella approached him and charmed him. She is very beautiful and persuasive. She made promises of wealth, power, and glory. Many think that she is the actual mastermind behind Queen Kathelina's movements."

"You see, Queen Kathelina was not always a bad person. She was gifted the northwest corner of Annabellia, and a castle was constructed for her centuries ago by one of our great kings. She lived in harmony with generations of Annabellians. There are even stories of her often visiting the castle of Lordstown and sharing meals and attending parties held by our royalty. But with the crowning of Princess Gabriella came greed and an evil hunger for more land and power. It is the king's belief that Princess Gabriella wants to rule Kathelina's castle, and Queen Kathelina wants to take over the castle of Lordstown."

"Where did Princess Gabriella come from?" I asked.

Mitchell answered, "She is the queen's only daughter. She was a sweet child, but something changed when she was crowned a princess. The reality is that Queen Kathelina has not aged for centuries, so Gabriella will never be the queen of the northwest castle. Shortly after being named a princess, her father, Queen Kathelina's husband—King William—mysteriously passed away. Many think that he was poisoned by the princess herself. You see, King William was a grateful, peace-loving man. He would never have condoned an attack on the people of Annabellia or the castle of Lordstown. As a matter of fact, before Gabriella was a princess, they didn't even have an army. With her father gone and the army that she started growing in strength and numbers, she seems to have gotten into the head of her mother. She has convinced Queen Kathelina that she deserves the castle of Lordstown because she is the most powerful person in Annabellia. This in turn would make Princess Gabriella queen of their castle."

Mitchell saw the concern in my face. I started to speak again, but he cut me off. "Don't worry, Daniel. I will never leave your side. I promise to keep you safe. Always remember that you have the magic and you hold tremendous power. The queen's disciples and soldiers will know this as well. Most importantly, I promise you that good old Mitchell will be with you the whole time. Now time to teach you some of that magic. Grab Wanda," Mitchell commanded. I pulled the wand out of the holder. "Point it at that plant, flick your wrist, and repeat after me: Za-ru-na, Zaruna."

I pointed Wanda at the potted plant. Well, it was more of a small leafless, lifeless tree in a pot. Then I flicked my wrist and said, "Zaruna." Nothing happened. Mitchell let out a sigh and shook his head looking at the ground.

"You have to speak and flick at the same time, Daniel." He definitely sounded frustrated, and I became a little defensive.

"How am I supposed to know that? I did exactly what you told me to do!"

"Okay, okay, Daniel, you are right. Now watch me." He pointed his stick at the plant and simultaneously said, "Zaruna" as he flicked his wrist.

"It didn't work." I had stated the obvious.

With another sigh, Mitchell said, "Of course it didn't, Daniel. I don't have powers in Annabellia. Remember?" I recalled the conversation and nodded sheepishly. "Now try again please."

I held out my wand and commanded, "Zaruna!" A flash of light shot out of my wand with so much force that it almost knocked me out of my desk. The light was jagged, like a lightning bolt with a round fireball at its end. The flaming ball hit the potted plant and *bam*! The noise was deafening. The pot and plant disintegrated instantly; dirt sprinkled the room, with some hitting my face and landing on my head. Within seconds, the powerful light was gone; and the room was silent, except for the sound of the falling dirt hitting the floor.

Cowering in the corner, Mitchell looked up through his arms, which were covering his head, and exclaimed, "Holy mother of...what the...how in the world!" Mitchell seemed to be losing his mind. "My house!" he screamed and ran to where the pot had been. The plant was gone, and there was now a hole in the tree wall about the size of a basketball. It was charred and smoking. Mitchell looked through the hole, and he could see outside. There was another tree right next door to his, and it also had a smoldering hole through it. "I have never seen anything like that in my entire life." He sat down, looking baffled and exhausted at the same time. He was silent and perplexed, and I was uncomfortable.

"I'm sorry" was all I could say, and I didn't even know if that was an appropriate response. But I felt like I needed to break the silence. Slowly, Mitchell turned his head and looked me square in the eyes.

"Daniel?" Mitchell said with a questioning tone in his voice. "Do you happen to know what time you were born?" He was out of breath, and his head was now facing the floor. But his eyes were still locked on mine.

"Ten ten in the morning," I said with a confused tone in my voice. I knew this because my mom always talked about and loved to tell everyone about the coincidence. I think I was the only kid in my class that knew the exact time of their birth.

"Holy cr—oh my go—" He spoke slowly. "Ten ten in the morning on October 10? I don't believe this! Ten-ten-ten-ten and today you are ten! It's the perfect birthday! The king will be so excited. We must leave now."

"I thought you were going to train me before we left," I stated, concerned.

"Ha ha!" Mitchell scoffed. "I am not qualified to train someone with a perfect birthday. That is something only the king can do. When he hears of this, he will want us at the castle immediately."

Chapter 7

Mitchell was frantic. He went to one of the empty desks, sat down, and quickly scribbled a short paragraph on a piece of paper. I couldn't read what he had written because it was messy and he was too far away from me. He rolled up the paper, tied a string around it, and said, "Follow me." We climbed down the spiral staircase to the kitchen. Mitchell scurried to the birdcage in the corner of the room and opened its small door. He reached his hand in and called out, "C'mon, Christine." The small black bird crawled onto his open left palm. He held the note out right in front of the bird's eyes. "Take this to King Salvatore immediately." The bird grabbed the paper and flew out a small open window over the sink.

"Whoa!" I gasped. "Does he really know where he's going?"

"Yes," Mitchell answered. He then continued, a bit annoyed, "*She* knows exactly where *she* is going. Now we must pack." He looked over at me, and then raised his voice with a tone that was somewhere between anger and panic. "Where is Wanda?" I cocked my head a little but didn't answer. "Your wand! Where is your wand!"

"Up…stairs," I answered sheepishly.

"Go get it now, and I mean it when I say never to walk away from it again!"

I scrambled up the stairs, grabbed Wanda, and came back down. By the time I returned, Mitchell had a small suitcase out on the kitchen table with a pair of socks already packed. "Here! Put this on." Mitchell tossed a leather belt to me. "This is for Wanda." I studied the belt a little closer. It had a sleeve with a snap on the top. "Stow the wand whenever you aren't using it. It should either be in your hand or on your belt—nowhere else."

I acknowledged Mitchell with an understanding nod.

"We will leave immediately," he stated with a no-nonsense tone in his voice. "We should make it about halfway if we leave now. That will put us at the castle tomorrow afternoon." He looked at me from head to toe. "You will have to wear what you have on since I don't have any other clothes that will fit you." Mitchell pointed at a faded blue-and-yellow checkered backpack in the corner of the room and commanded, "Grab that, Daniel. There is a tent, a couple of wooden plates, utensils, and some snacks inside. We will stop for dinner at Martha's home. She is a great cook and always accepts company. Hopefully she will be making her famous braslowberry pie!"

"Braslowberry pie?" I said slowly, making sure that I was pronouncing it correctly.

"Ah yes, you are not lucky enough to have braslowberries in your world. Do you like blueberries?" Mitchell asked. I nodded. "Well, they're nothing like that." He laughed. I guess he thought that was funny. I gave him half a smirk and a small fake chuckle. He continued, "They're nothing like strawberries or blackberries or any berry that you would know. They're more like…well…I don't know, but we will be passing many braslowberry trees. And you can decide for yourself what they are like."

Mitchell looked around, grabbed his tiny suitcase and a small walking stick, and said, "Let's go." He nodded to the door, and I pushed it open with my left hand and walked out with Wanda in my right hand and the backpack slung over my left shoulder. He followed me, turned around, put his walking stick in the hole next to the door, twisted it, and the door closed.

"Go west, young man!" he barked with a smile like he just said something clever. I looked at him, confused, and didn't say a word. Mitchell sighed disappointedly and said, "Okay, then, follow me." He waved his arm in that already-familiar "come along" motion and started walking.

I looked ahead as we began marching toward that beautiful waterfall I had seen when I first entered Annabellia. I hoped that we would pass it, but I kept the thought to myself. By this time, Mitchell was already about ten feet in front of me, so I hurried to catch up. Within seconds, I was on Mitchell's left side. He looked up at me, and with an excited tone in his voice and a smile on his face, he said, "Get ready for an adventure for the ages!"

CHAPTER 8

We walked for an hour or so over mostly green pastures with some small rolling hills. Beautifully colored birds and butterflies swooped and fluttered everywhere. Some even seemed to follow us for a while. Mitchell was using his walking stick as an aid for every step that he took with his right foot. He had been surprisingly quiet for the first part of our journey, speaking every once in a while only to point out a specific flower or bird. When he did speak, he seemed to be a little short of breath. I had a feeling the walk wasn't easy for him.

We were getting close to the majestic waterfall—a torrent of the bluest water that I had ever seen. As we approached the beautiful sight, I couldn't take my eyes off it. The water was pouring over the edge of a mountain and breaking up into several separate streams as it hit giant boulders on its way down. The constant crash into the pool below was nearly deafening. Mitchell spoke in a voice that was almost a yell in an attempt to overpower the noise from the waterfall. "We will rest here awhile and have lunch." I nodded. "Right over there." He pointed to a circle of rocks that formed what looked to be a fire ring with two small stone benches on either side. We walked over, and Mitchell sat on one of the benches. We were now far enough away from the waterfall that we didn't have to shout. However, we were still close enough to feel the mist in the atmosphere. "Gather some firewood and bring it back here." He pointed away from the waterfall at a cluster of about five trees. "There should be plenty of sticks under those braslowberry trees."

"Braslowberry?" I asked and looked high up into the trees. They were a little ways away, but there seemed to be a bunch of pinkish-purple volleyballs hanging from the branches.

"Yes, those are braslowberry trees," Mitchell answered, "and keep your eyes up because you don't want one of those things falling on your head."

I nodded and walked over to the trees. As I got closer, I could see that the braslowberries were, indeed, about the size of volleyballs. There were a few smashed on the ground, and the inside of the fruit was a deep dark purple with big black seeds scattered throughout. I stepped around the smashed fruit, picking up as many sticks as I could carry and started walking back.

"Wait!" Mitchell called. He stood up and started walking toward me. "Drop those sticks!" I did as he said, and they fell to the ground in a messy pile. As he approached me, he said, "Let's try something. Take Wanda, and as you point in a circle around the sticks, say 'walketh.'"

"Walketh?" I said, confused.

"Yes, 'walketh,'" he continued. "Not all your magic has cool words like *zaruna*!"

I removed Wanda from the leather sleeve and pointed the wand at the pile of wood. I started to make a circle around the pile of sticks and exclaimed, "Walketh!" Magically, the sticks came together and formed a tidy pile shaped like a dog and about the size of a suitcase.

"Now walk to the firepit," Mitchell commanded with a big smile on his face like he was surprised that it worked. I started walking to the ring and benches. I looked over my shoulder, and incredibly, the sticks were following me. As we came to the firepit, Mitchell motioned for me to bend over so he could whisper something to me. "Say 'entereth' with a flick toward the firepit, and then say 'falleth' with a second one."

"Entereth," I commanded as I pointed to the firepit, and the stick dog climbed over the rocks. With another flick, "Falleth," I said, and the sticks tumbled into a pile in the middle of the fire ring. "Unbelievable!" I screamed, wide-eyed. "That was awesome!"

"That was awesome," Mitchell stated loudly, half because he was excited and half because he was talking over the waterfall. "I have never seen that work the first time for anybody." He looked at me. "Now we are going to practice control. Do you remember what happened when you used the zaruna spell?"

"Yes," I answered.

"Well, we will not be doing that anytime soon. I want you to scale back that power. You are going to flick at those sticks and just say 'za.' If you say 'zaruna,' you will blast the pile to kingdom come, so just say 'za.'"

I held Wanda out in front of me, and with a flick of the wrist—"Za." A much smaller yellow flash came out of the tip with a small flaming ball at the end. The ball hit the sticks and broke like a fiery water balloon around the sticks. Fire ignited all the kindling, and we had a campfire just like that.

Mitchell sat on the ground and stretched his legs out. He clasped his hands together behind his head and rested his head against one of the stone benches. He had a satisfied smile on his face as he let out an "Ahhhhh." He added, "I can get used to having you around." Mitchell pulled his hat over his eyes and continued, "Now walk down to the stream, give Wanda a flick, and say 'fish-soloeth.' It is important that you say the word *soloeth* because that means 'one.' And since the word *fish* is both singular and plural, well, you don't want to see what would happen if you didn't put a number on it."

I walked down to the bank of the stream. "Fish-soloeth," I said with a flick of the wrist as I pointed Wanda at the river. A small light left Wanda's tip and hit the stream below. *Whoosh!* A big splash of water shot up like a geyser, and from the middle, a big bright-yellow fish came flying out of the stream. It went up about fifty feet and was headed in my direction, hurtling through the air right at me. I put both arms over my head and ducked. *Thud!* The fish hit me right on the arms. It would have been my head if I hadn't covered up. I heard a chuckle from Mitchell's direction. He had pulled his hat up just far enough to see the show and was smiling broadly. "Very funny!" I yelled as I picked the fish up and returned to the fire. The fish was big, maybe two feet in length, and had some girth to it. It would definitely be enough to feed us both.

"Set the fish down, and with a flick, say 'cooketh,'" Mitchell instructed.

I did as he said; and the fish lifted into the air, slowly floated about a foot above the fire, and began spinning slowly like it was on an invisible roaster.

"Wow," I said under my breath, "this will never get old."

Mitchell stood up and said, "I'll grab the dishes out of the backpack. While the fish is cooking, you go get us a fruit for dessert." He pointed to the braslowberry trees.

I nodded and walked back over to the trees. He didn't tell me how to retrieve the fruit; maybe he forgot. But I was pretty sure that I would just have to add "eth" to anything I wanted Wanda to get me. I pointed at a braslowberry, flicked my wrist, and said "Fruiteth!" Why I used the word *fruit* instead of *braslowberry*, I had no idea. Maybe because *fruit* was the last thing that Mitchell called it. Well, I immediately discovered that I should have said "soloeth" or "braslowberry" because all five trees, as well as the ground, started to shake. Every branch on every tree was trembling.

"Daniel, look out!" Mitchell screamed.

One of the volleyball-sized fruits broke free and flew toward me. I turned around and started to run. When I looked back, there was an entire angry flock of braslowberries rocketing toward me. I was running as fast as I could, but the fruit was getting closer.

"Get under the water!" Mitchell screamed from the firepit. I ran to the bank of the river and, without slowing down, launched myself off the edge like an Olympic long jumper, running through the air before landing feetfirst into the water. I torpedoed underwater about five feet down. I looked up and could see the braslowberries bombarding the surface of the water in a mad flurry. Luckily, the fruit only dove about a foot under the surface before it harmlessly bobbed back up and started to float. I stayed under the water for what seemed like forever, but I'm sure it was only about twenty seconds. When I finally saw what I assumed was the last braslowberry splashing into the water, I waited another five seconds or so, and then swam to the surface.

I pushed a couple of pieces of fruit aside and stuck my head above the water. I looked around and saw hundreds of braslowberries bobbing in the water all around me. I looked back to the bank; and Mitchell was standing there looking, studying me.

Once he figured I was okay, he smiled and said, "You forgot to say 'soloeth,' didn't ya?" I was treading water and nodded. All of the sudden, with a look of panic on his face, he cried, "Oh no! Where's Wanda?"

Still treading water, I held the wand out of the water with my right hand.

"That's my boy!" Mitchell said, relieved and proud. I swam back to shore in just a few strokes. "Grab a berry," Mitchell said with a smile on his face. "Do you know where you might find any?"

I rolled my eyes and grabbed the closest piece of fruit. It was neither hard nor soft but kind of heavy and definitely something that you would not want to get hit by. I crawled out of the water and climbed up the bank.

By the time I made it back to the firepit, Mitchell had put the cooked fish on both our plates. I set the braslowberry down and, soaking wet, sat on the stone bench where my plate was. Thankfully, it was not cold outside, but I was definitely not comfortable in my wet clothes. I took my wooden fork and cut a small piece of fish. I lifted it up. It had a bluish tint, so I was a little nervous about the taste. Nevertheless, I was so hungry that I slowly put the fork to my mouth and took an initial bite.

Now, my dad used to take me fishing on Lake Erie all the time. And I never thought I would taste fish that was better than good old Lake Erie walleye, but this blue fish was insane. Not only was this the best fish that I had ever tasted, but it was the best-tasting piece of meat I had ever eaten. I can't even explain what it tasted like. It wasn't sweet. It wasn't salty. It wasn't tart or spicy or tangy. It was just awesome. I savored the rest of my fish over the next five minutes. Then I let out a large belch, moved off the bench onto the ground, and lay next to the fire. My clothes were still wet, but I barely noticed because my belly was never happier.

"Let's take five," Mitchell said, but I had already closed my eyes.

Chapter 9

"Daniel, wake up." I heard a quiet whisper and felt someone shaking my shoulder. "Daniel, we need to get going." I looked up through my barely opened eyes and saw Mitchell standing over me.

"How long was I asleep?" I asked groggily as the reality sunk in that I really was in Annabellia and not in my own bed at home just outside of Cleveland. I felt like I had been asleep for days.

"Fifteen minutes," Mitchell answered. "I gave you an extra ten because you looked so peaceful."

I sat up, looked around, and let everything sink in again. He must've been telling the truth about the fifteen minutes because my clothes were still damp.

"Here," he said, "have some dessert," and he held out a plate with bite-size chunks of braslowberries on it.

I reached out, grabbed a piece, and studied it. Mitchell must have removed the big black seeds from the dark-purple fruit. I popped the piece into my mouth. "Wow!" I exclaimed with the fruit still in my mouth. "This is amazing!" It was juicy, sweet, and salty. It even had a little heat to it, but it worked. If all the food in Annabellia was as good as that fish and this fruit, well, I was in for a real treat!

"Don't talk with your mouth full," Mitchell said with a smile because he really didn't mean it. "We need to leave now if we want to get to Martha's house in time for dinner." I stood up, nodded, and grabbed three more pieces of braslowberry with my left hand. I popped another piece of fruit in my mouth, and Mitchell pointed at the fire. "Give her a flick and say 'drowneth.'"

I did as he said and *whoosh*! A big—I don't know how to explain it—blob, maybe, of water lifted from the stream, floated over the fire, and then just dropped on the firepit, instantly drenching and extinguishing the campfire.

Mitchell rubbed his hands together, grabbed his cane, and ordered, "Grab the backpack, put those plates in there, and let's go." He pointed to the two clean wooden plates sitting on one of the benches. He must have rinsed them off in the river. I grabbed the plates, put them in the backpack, and hurried to catch up to him as he was already off, walking at a brisk pace.

"How long until we get to Martha's?" I asked.

"Should be less than two hours." He paused. "Unless—"

"Unless what?" I interrupted.

"Unless the lolosters are out."

"What are lolosters?" I asked, intrigued and a bit scared.

"I guess you would probably describe them as dragons. However, they don't look like dinosaurs or giant lizards. They look like enormous birds. Most of them are black, but sometimes you will see a blue or red one. They breathe fire, and they are carnivorous. Their favorite food is animals that are, well, about our size. They are big birds, so big that they can only fly short distances before getting tired. That being said, they are extremely fast." I looked at Mitchell, and he shrugged his shoulders in a "just sayin'" kind of way. "When we cross the skinny bridge of Dee Dee, we enter their territory. They live in caves high up on the mountains of Magnolia. They actually see better at night, so it's good that we will get there in daylight. Most of them sleep until sunset. However, sometimes, when it is light out, we will encounter one or two from time to time. That being said, Daniel, with my wit and experience, I have no doubt that we can easily get past a couple. I've done it dozens of times before." He paused, and then added, "Let's just hope there's not more than a couple." Wide-eyed, I looked at him, but he was looking straight ahead like he was done talking about it.

As we walked a little in silence, I noticed we were approaching some mountains. Mitchell spoke, "See up ahead?" He pointed with his walking stick. I squinted and remained quiet because I wasn't sure what he was pointing at. "Those are the mountains of Magnolia. And straight ahead is the skinny bridge of Dee Dee, which leads to Dee Dee's Dark Wood Forest. It is named after one of the great queens of the past. And it's called Dark Woods because the woods are so dense that in the middle of the day, it feels like dusk."

I squinted. I could barely make out the bridge, but I could easily see the mountains. And there definitely was what appeared to be a dense forest between them. We continued on for another ten minutes or so. The mountains grew larger, but then started to disappear behind the thick forest that Mitchell had mentioned earlier. We approached the bridge, and Mitchell stopped. "Okay, Daniel, this is where we cross into loloster territory. After we cross the bridge, the woods will give us cover from the lolosters."

As we reached the entrance of the bridge, I peered down. We must have been two hundred feet above a river. The walls of the surrounding canyon were steep and sheer, and jagged rocks pierced the roiling water far below. The bridge itself was a rotting heap of brown rope and wooden planks. It was probably about a hundred feet long, but it seemed more like a thousand. The bridge sagged in the middle. Its rope looked to be frayed in some spots, and there were more than a few planks missing.

"Are you sure this is safe?" I murmured.

"Yes, Daniel," Mitchell replied confidently, "I've been across this bridge a million times."

"Can't I use Wanda to fix it and make it stronger?" I thought this was a great idea.

"No, Daniel, we can't take that chance. If something goes wrong, the bridge may break, fall, and be gone forever."

"Can Wanda help us fly across?" I sounded desperate, but I thought that was another fair question.

"Ha ha, no, Daniel. Wanda cannot make you fly." Mitchell grabbed the rope with his left hand and started to cross the bridge, still using his cane for support. I stood at the edge as Mitchell wobbled farther away from me. He turned around and claimed, "See Daniel, it's all good." Feeling defeated, I grabbed onto the rope and took my first step.

Chapter 10

Mitchell was about halfway across the rickety bridge when I took my second tentative step. Then I began pushing forward. I had Wanda in my right hand; and I slid her along the top support, trying to maintain constant contact with the rope handrail. I slid my left hand along the other side as well. I concentrated on the planks, making sure I didn't step where one was missing. I sensed that Mitchell kept looking back to check on me, but there was no way I was taking my eyes off where my feet were going. Every once in a while, I would hear him shout words of encouragement, but I was terrified and moving painfully slow.

I was about halfway across, where the bridge sagged down the farthest, when I heard a horrible noise. It was a fast hissing or sizzling sound. The rope was unraveling! *Snap!* The right side of the bridge let go. The planks went out from underneath my feet and swung under the left side of the bridge. As I clung to the handrail rope on the left, I somehow managed to get both my feet to the bottom rope on the left side. My right arm was flailing with nothing to hold on to. "Daniel!" Mitchell yelled from the edge of the cliff. "Hang on!"

I looked up at my left hand and immediately realized I had to get my right hand onto that rope. I thought about dropping the wand, but for some reason, I just couldn't. I looked down and saw the backpack disappear into the rocky river hundreds of feet below. I swung my body up with all my effort and was able to grab onto the rope without dropping Wanda. I now stood on the bottom rope with both hands on the top. I looked down. I looked back. I looked at Mitchell. The time for moving slowly was over.

I shimmied over the second half of the bridge, never lifting my feet or hands off the rope. I must've covered the second half of that bridge in seconds. As I approached the end, Mitchell reached out with his little arms and grabbed my shirt and pulled as I leaped off what was left of the bridge. I landed on top of him. He put his arms around me and patted me on the back. "Nice work," he grunted as he struggled to breathe under my weight. I rolled off him and looked up at the sky. We both lay on our backs next to each other. "That was a close one," Mitchell sighed.

"Ya think?" I snapped, still short of breath.

We lay there for a while, trying to digest what had just happened. "You okay?" Mitchell asked.

"I guess," I answered in a whisper.

Mitchell stood up. "Okay, Daniel, we need to get moving."

I rolled onto my knees and stood up slowly. I looked over my shoulder at the bridge that had almost ended me, I took a step in the direction that we were about to travel. "Stop!" Mitchell commanded loudly. Then his voice softened. "I want to try something." I looked at him, and he said, "Point Wanda at the bridge, make a big circle, flick at the bridge, and yell 'repaireth.' Now, I'm not talking a flick of the wrist this time. Flick with your entire arm."

I stepped near the edge of the cliff, made a big circle with my arm, and forcefully thrust it at the bridge. "Repaireth!" I yelled. The bridge began to sparkle from side to side. Rope began to twist. Planks seemed to appear from thin air, and *bam bam bam* echoed throughout the canyon. There was so much light that I was forced to squint, so I could barely see what was happening. With one last loud *zap*, the bridge reappeared—in perfect shape. There wasn't a single missing plank, and the rope looked brand new. "You have got to be kidding me!" I yelled in the direction of Mitchell while never taking my eyes off the beautiful bridge I had just built.

"Heh heh." Mitchell chuckled. "I guess it did work. Who knew?"

I was still angry, thinking about how close to death I had come just a few minutes ago. "Why in the world did you make me cross that old bridge? I almost died!"

"I'm sorry," Mitchell said sheepishly. "But there was a chance that you would have destroyed the bridge before we crossed it. Now that we successfully made it to the other side, I figured we had nothing to lose since the bridge was in scattered pieces anyway, and it would have been impossible to cross it as it was." He paused and admired my work for a minute. "Shall we continue on?" he asked as if I actually had a choice.

"Fine," I answered in an angry tone.

"Daniel," Mitchell said quietly, "can you do me one more favor?"

I looked at him, annoyed. "What?" I barked.

"Can you make that same motion at the bridge with Wanda, but this time, say 'strength-increaseth?'"

I grudgingly walked over to the bridge, whipped my arm in a giant circle, and yelled, "Strength-increaseth!" Silence. Nothing happened, and I looked at Mitchell. He shrugged his shoulders and gave me the familiar "c'mon" wave of his arm. We took about two steps when from behind us, we heard an explosion which almost knocked us over. We both ducked and covered our heads. When I finally turned around, I saw a blinding light flash from the direction of the bridge. The light was accompanied by the loudest, longest roar of thunder that I had ever heard. It must've lasted a minute, and then abruptly stopped.

There was smoke everywhere. As it began to dissipate, the bridge came into sight. It was no longer a rope bridge with wooden planks. It was now a shiny steel bridge with a cover and walls. The bridge had supports coming out of the cliffs, and instead of sagging, it had a slight arch in the middle. It was not wide enough for a car, but no doubt, it was strong enough for one.

"Oh, come on!" I yelled. "Seriously? You made me cross that old bridge, and I could've done this first?" I glared at Mitchell, waiting for a response.

"Sorry, Danny. I have never worked with an apprentice with your powers." He shrugged his shoulders again. "I couldn't take the chance." He looked at me for acknowledgment or forgiveness or acceptance or, well, something. Maybe it was because he called me "Danny," or maybe it was because he said I was powerful, but I instantly felt the desire to move forward and hold no grudges. I gave him a little smile and a nod. He seemed relieved.

"That's my boy! Me and Danny moving on!" I looked at the ground and smiled again. I didn't know why, but I really liked it when he called me Danny.

"Forward march!" Mitchell commanded with a rejuvenated tone in his voice.

Chapter 11

We left the bridge and entered the dense forest filled with giant trees. "Welcome to Dee Dee's Dark Wood Forest," Mitchell said as we followed a footpath which snaked around an army of enormous trunks. The trees looked like the one that Mitchell lived in. Most of the branches were up high, but there were so many and they were so thick that most of the sunlight was blocked. It was still bright enough that we could see the path, but it looked and felt like early evening. It was kind of spooky.

"Is there anything dangerous in here?" I asked in a nervous tone.

"No, Daniel. These woods are safe."

"Phew!" I replied.

Mitchell quickly continued, "Well, it's safe during the day when the lolosters are resting." I looked at him, cross-eyed, but he looked straight ahead. We continued burrowing through the dark forest for a few more minutes when we finally began to see the light getting brighter through the trees. We were close to the edge of the woods when Mitchell put his cane in front of my chest. "Stop right here," he ordered. He hunched over and crept toward the last tree. He put both arms on the trunk and leaned to his right, peeking around it. Then he looked skyward. "Oh no." He sighed. "I was afraid of that." He turned around so that his back was touching the tree, and he was facing me. Defeated, he slid down into a seated position and put his hands over his face, which was now turned to the ground.

"What's wrong?" I asked, agitated and curious. "What's going on, Mitchell? What do you see?"

Mitchell sighed again and drew a long slow breath. He looked up at me. "Come here, Daniel." I slowly made my way to the tree he was sitting against. "Carefully and slowly, peek around this tree and look up to the mountains."

I did as he said. When I lifted my eyes to the sky and looked to the mountains off in the distance, I saw dozens of giant, well, I would say dragons, but Mitchell called them lolosters. I looked ahead and saw nothing but a narrow green pasture—no trees, no rocks, no shrubs, just grass. Just grass and what looked like a line of igloos which stretched the entire length of the field in a straight row. The last one sat near to where the woods began again—about, I don't know, two football fields away, maybe. It wasn't terribly far, but it was definitely more than a stone's throw.

A line of jagged mountains with caves bored into their sides skied above both sides of the field. Ominously, the lolosters circled overhead.

I came back around to the safe side of the tree. "I thought you said they slept all day. You said we may see just a couple! There must be fifty of them flying around up there!" I was scared. I was frustrated. I was confused. I wanted answers.

"It must've been the commotion that we made at the bridge. That noise was so loud. That has to be why they are all awake. Oh, how are we going to get past them?" Mitchell may have answered my question, but I'm pretty sure he was just thinking out loud.

"Why don't we camp in the woods overnight, and we can cross in the morning?" I asked with conviction.

"No, no, no, no, Daniel! We can't. You see, the lolosters fly down at night and enter the woods to look for food. We have to cross today. We have to cross now."

The panic in his voice alarmed me. Mitchell sat silently for a minute or two, and then rolled onto his stomach and crawled around the tree to the edge of the pasture. "Come here, Daniel." I got down on my stomach and army-crawled up next to him. "You see that line of huts?" And with his cane, he pointed to the igloos that dotted the field.

"Uh-huh," I answered.

"They are exactly one hundred feet apart from one another. Our ancestors put them there generations ago. They have small doors on both ends facing the woods and unbreakable fireproof windows on the roof and on both sides facing the mountains. We use these to get across the field.

"One, two, three, four, five, six," I counted out loud, pointing to each of the huts.

"Yes, six. We should be able to get to the first one no problem. Maybe the second one too. But after that, we will be tempting fate. You see, if they catch sight of us, they can be on the ground in seconds. That's why it's usually easy to cross during the day. If there's only one or two out flying around, it's easy to cross when they aren't looking. Most times we can make it all the way across without being noticed even once."

I looked up and watched the giant birds. Many of them were now sitting on ledges outside the caves. Others were wheeling in circles just off the ledges. Most of them were black, but there were two red ones and a blue one. Not bright colors—dull and dark, almost black themselves. I watched one take off and circle twice before it returned to the ledge. I tried to count them, but there were too many.

"Okay, Danny, here's the plan. We are going to slowly crawl on our bellies to the first hut. If you hear me yell, 'now,' get up and run. Do not go back to the woods—even if it is closer—because they will follow you in. As soon as we are inside the hut, we must close the doors because if they are chasing us, they will breathe fire."

"What about zaruna? Can I zaruna their butts?"

"Daniel, they breathe fire," Mitchell said like that was the stupidest suggestion that he had ever heard. "They would eat your fireballs like a snack and burp smoke when they're done."

"What about water? Does Wanda have a water spell?"

"Wanda can shoot water, but the stream from the wand would be no match for the amount of fire that the lolosters breathe." Mitchell paused. "There is one possibility, but the only human I know who has ever done it successfully is the evil queen."

"What is it?" I asked.

"It's like a force field. The magic word is *protecteth*. You have surprised me so far, Daniel, but we cannot rely on it."

I stood up behind the tree and…"Protecteth!" I said with a flick and my arm straight up. Nothing happened.

"Keep quiet, Daniel, you will give us away. The spell won't work unless you actually need to be protected. Now get back on the ground."

I dropped back down to my knees and sheepishly slithered up next to Mitchell. "You ready?" he asked. I nodded. "Follow me and be ready to run." Mitchell began squirming on his stomach toward the first hut. I was directly behind him with my face almost rubbing against the soles of his tiny shoes. We both kept our eyes on the sky, peeking at the hut now, and then to make sure we were headed straight at it. The lolosters were still off in the distance, and the ones that were flying were not going too far from the ledge. I noticed some sitting on the ledge, glaring downward, but they did not appear to be looking in our direction.

After a long nervous army crawl, we arrived at the first hut, and its door was open. We scooted in, and Mitchell quietly closed the door behind us. The door that was in front of us was also open; so Mitchell slowly closed that one too, exclaiming, "That wasn't so bad now, was it?" I looked up through the glass and could see the giant birds soaring in the distance. He added, "Now, when we leave, we must leave the doors open for the next travelers. You see, the last thing you want to have to do when you are trying to avoid a loloster is fumble around trying to open a door." That made sense, and I nodded.

"So when we leave this hut, do not close the door behind you."

"Okay," I responded.

Mitchell put his hands on the window facing the left mountain and looked up. He turned around and did the same on the right window. I was looking through the roof window and saw that the lolosters were still beyond us and beyond the second hut as well. But by the time we would get to the third and fourth huts, we would be directly underneath them.

"Okay, Danny, we are going to change it up a bit for round 2." I looked at him, waiting for orders. "There is a good chance one—or more—will see us this time. We are going to crawl on our hands and knees, not our stomachs. We need to be ready to run." Mitchell said, "One, two, three," and he began crawling out of the hut on his hands and knees. Again, I followed him right on his heels. He was slow and methodical at first, but he then began to pick up his pace. We kept our eyes on the sky just as we did the first time. We were a little more than halfway when I looked at the hut and...

"NOW!" I looked up, and Mitchell was running to the open door. I glanced up at the sky, and a loloster, the blue one, had broken the circle formation and was diving in our direction. I popped up to my feet and took off. I blew past Mitchell about ten steps from the door, and then slid feetfirst through the doorway like I was sliding into home plate. I skidded past the first door; and my feet hit the second door, slamming it shut. I looked behind me; and Mitchell, in one motion, ran through the doorway at full speed, grabbed the first door, and slammed it behind him. He tried to hit the brakes, but he slammed into me. Most of his momentum had stopped. So I just kinda grabbed him, and we softly fell to the ground. I looked up through the ceiling and saw the dark-blue winged monster fly back into the sky.

"Will he be waiting for us now?" I asked, panicked.

"No, Daniel. Remember, they don't see well during the day. He probably didn't even know what he was chasing."

"Okay," I answered, only half-believing him.

"Now it's gonna get dicey, Daniel."

Now? I thought but didn't say anything.

"Like I said, when they are circling like this or sitting on the ledge, one or more will be facing our direction. This time on three, we are just going to run for it. You will get there first, so close the far door when you get there and be ready to close the second one as soon as I arrive. Are you ready?" I nodded. "One, two, three!"

Mitchell took two steps; and I was by him, running faster than I ever had. After I passed him, I heard a loud squawk. When I looked up, I saw a loloster that was sitting on the cliff to the right roll his head and kind of fall off the ledge. Within a second or two, the streamlined dragon-like bird was screaming toward us like a missile. A couple more were tailing him down. He was getting close, but I knew I could beat him. Just then, he let out more of a roar than a squawk, and a stream of fire blazed toward me. I was at the doorway when the fire blasted into the roof of the igloo and deflected skyward. I slammed the far door and turned back to see Mitchell still about twenty yards away. The loloster that missed me was already soaring upward, but the ones that had followed it were going to take their shot at Mitchell. I sprinted to the door, holding it with my right hand and gripping Wanda in my left.

ANNABELLIA

"C'mon, Mitchell! Hurry up!" I screamed just as I heard a roar and saw a bolt of fire spearing in Mitchell's direction. "Protecteth!" I yelled as I flicked my wrist with authority. The fire stream continued blazing toward Mitchell without any interference. He was leaning back as the fire struck his hat. It knocked the hat off his head, disintegrating it instantly in a ball of fire. Mitchell was still able to snap his body forward and somersault into the hut as I slammed the door behind him. He ended up on his back with his arms and legs straight out. He was breathing heavily, and his round belly was pumping up and down so fast it was almost blurry. I looked down at his beet-red face and his bald head. "Are you all right, Mitchell?"

"Yeah…I…guess…protecteth…didn't…work," he said breathlessly. How…are…we…going to…get…to 4?"

We sat in silence for a minute, and I finally said, "What if I create a distraction?"

Mitchell was catching his breath. "How do you mean?" He was able to spit out before taking a big gulp of air.

"Well, you said I can't use zaruna because fire doesn't hurt them, right?" Mitchell nodded. "What if I shot a fireball at the base of the cliff? Wouldn't they chase that?"

Mitchell thought for a second. "That is brilliant, Danny boy!" He sounded like a proud papa. "Here's what we're gonna do. Remember zaruna almost knocked you over and za was just enough to start a campfire, so we are going to go with zaru. We don't want the lolosters flying over us, so we will need two fireballs behind us in both directions. Aim for something flammable so that the fire doesn't disappear when it hits the rock." Mitchell looked out the windows behind us. "There is a shrub on the left at the base of the north mountain and a small tree on the right about twenty feet up on the south one. If you shoot through the back doorway, they should be easy to hit. When you fire your first shot, I will take off. Fire your second and get out as soon as you can. Remember to leave both doors open."

As Mitchell readied himself at the front doorway, I positioned myself at the back door. I aimed Wanda and shouted, "Zaru!" The shot sent a fireball diagonally out of the doorway, blasting the shrub that Mitchell had pointed out. The explosion must have startled and caught the attention of the giant birds, and they all began squawking loudly. It was like they were yelling to one another. The lolosters on the north cliff started diving toward the fire. I looked the other way, and—"Zaru!" Bull's-eye! The tree twenty feet up became an instant inferno. The lolosters from the south began screaming and immediately dove to investigate. I turned around and ran out the front door.

I must've shot those fireballs much faster than I thought because I was barely halfway to the next hut and I was already flying by Mitchell. His little legs were churning, but he wasn't going very fast. As I ran into the fourth hut, we seemed to have been unnoticed. I waited a few more seconds, and Mitchell came huffing and puffing through the door. I breathlessly stated, "They have no idea! Let's keep going." Unable to talk, Mitchell nodded, looked up in both directions, and out the door he went. Mitchell was moving as fast as he could, which was pretty slow; so I kind of walked-ran backward behind him, making sure that we stayed unnoticed.

We reached the sixth hut. Mitchell was bent over with his hands on his knees, struggling for every breath. "We need to keep moving," I pleaded. Mitchell didn't look up. He just lifted his right arm and held out his index finger in a "wait a minute" gesture. I kept looking out. The lolosters were starting to lose interest in the fires. "We gotta go now!"

"Okay," he answered and sucked it up and made his way to the door. Using every ounce of energy he had left, he rocked once, twice, and scrambled out the door. His tiny legs were moving like little pistons, but again, he himself was not moving very fast or getting very far. I was jogging slowly behind him, looking over my shoulders in both directions, when I realized the lolosters were headed up to their ledges. They must have been tired because even if they had seen us, they no longer seemed interested in us. Before I knew it, we were crossing the threshold into the woods.

Mitchell continued about twenty steps into the woods and dropped to the ground. "We…did…it," he said, panting. "Great job…Danny!"

I lay down next to him, and we relaxed in silence for a while.

Finally, Mitchell complained, "That was my favorite hat! Now I have to see Martha looking like this." He sounded defeated.

The light went on in my head. "Aah, you like Martha, don't you?" I said in a teasing tone.

"Shut up, Daniel!" Mitchell said defensively.

"Mitchell and Martha sitting in a tree…k-i-s-s…"

"Shut up, Daniel!"

"Ohhhhh, she makes the best braslowberry…"

"Shut up, Daniel!" Mitchell stood up and, leaning heavily on his cane, started to walk briskly down a path between the trees. I followed closely behind him, making kissing noises and cracking myself up.

Chapter 12

We continued down the well-traveled path through the woods; and the trail soon led to an opening, revealing a small…village, I guess you would call it. There were about twenty small stone cottages, most of them with bright-colored shutters and doors. They all had stone chimneys, with smoke billowing out of almost every one of them. Villagers were milling about outside, and they all seemed cheerful and content. The men all wore pointed hats like the one that Mitchell lost, along with white shirts and suspenders. They all had white beards as well. The women wore sleeveless bright-colored dresses with white blouses. Shiny ribbons that matched their outfits held up buns in their gray hair. Everyone was short like Mitchell. Again, not to be offensive, but they all looked like gnomes. Nobody noticed us right away; but as we approached the cottages, I heard a man call loudly and happily, "Mitchell!"

Mitchell and I looked in the direction of the voice. "Franklin!" Mitchell shouted back. The man approached us quickly with a smile on his face and excitement in his eyes.

He stuck his hand out toward Mitchell and asked, "What brings you here, and who is your friend?"

Mitchell shook the man's hand vigorously. "This is Daniel, and we are on our way to see King Salvatore!"

Mitchell answered with pride in his voice. By this time, there was a lot of commotion, and several others were making their way over to us.

"Mitchell and I go way back," Franklin said to me as he shook my hand. "It is very nice to meet you, Daniel."

"Nice to meet you too, sir," I said, a bit overwhelmed.

"Sir!" Franklin exclaimed. "Ha ha, save your 'sirs' for King Salvatore!"

"Mitchell! Mitchell! Mitchell!" I kept hearing. I turned away from Franklin and saw Mitchell shaking lots of hands, hugging the women and calling them all by name.

"Will you be spending the night?" I heard someone ask.

"Yes," Mitchell answered, "I was going to see if Martha had room for us."

"Martha, of course," Franklin said with a chuckle.

Mitchell blushed. "Do you know if she is home?" He didn't direct the question at any one person but kind of to the whole group.

"Yes, yes. Of course she's home," answered one of the ladies.

"Thank you, Miss Dorothy," Mitchell said with a bow. "Come, Daniel," Mitchell ordered as we headed toward a cottage with sunny yellow shutters and a Kelly green door. Flowers brightened every window, and smoke rose from the chimney. Just as we were walking up a short stone path which led to the front door, it opened.

"Hi, Mitchell! I heard all the commotion and saw it was you. What a pleasant surprise."

Mitchell turned bright red, and he was looking at the ground. "Hi, Martha. It is nice to see you." Mitchell didn't even look up at her when he pointed at me and said, "This is Daniel. We are on our way to see the king, and we would be very grateful if we could rest here tonight." He finally raised his eyes toward Martha while his head was still facing down.

"Of course you may! You are always welcome! Could I interest you two in something to eat? I just started making dinner."

I was starving, but I didn't want to say anything. Mitchell looked at me, and I gave him a small nod. "Yes, that would be wonderful," Mitchell paused, and then added, "as long as it's not too much trouble."

"Not at all," Martha answered. "And after dinner, I will bake a braslowberry pie."

Mitchell looked at me and smiled. Martha invited us in, showed us to the kitchen table, and motioned for us to sit. We sat next to each other so we would both be facing Martha.

Martha looked at Mitchell. "I don't think I've ever seen you without a hat, Mitchell."

"Yes, I know. I lost my hat when it was destroyed by a loloster."

"Oh my goodness, Mitchell!" Martha gasped as she took a seat directly across the table. She put her elbows on the table, her chin in her palms, and looked into his eyes. "What happened?"

Mitchell gave her an abbreviated version of what happened but ended it with, "If it wasn't for Daniel, I don't think we would have made it."

Martha jumped up and hugged me. She caught me off guard. I was tense, and it probably felt like I didn't enjoy it.

But her head was in my chest. She was squeezing me tight, and the truth was, I did like it. Martha had a maternal feel to her. You could tell that she was kind, caring, and genuine. It was easy to see why Mitchell may have a crush on her, and I was beginning to think that the feeling was mutual.

We had a wonderful dinner. I sat silently most of the night, listening to those two talk about nothing and everything. I spoke only when one of them asked me a question directly. I didn't feel out of place. I just didn't have much to add, and I really enjoyed just listening to them.

Eventually, Martha got up and put a teapot on the stove and pulled the braslowberry pie out of the oven. It smelled so good that I couldn't wait to taste it. Soon the kettle was whistling, and Martha was pouring us tea and slicing up the pie. She put a slice in front of me, and then one in front of Mitchell. My mouth was watering from the aroma of the masterpiece on the table. Martha made her way to a drawer and pulled out a couple of wooden forks.

"I hope it's good," she said as she sat back down. She put her elbows on the table and rested her chin in her hands, looking at us like she couldn't wait for us to taste the pie. My fork went through the still-steaming dessert, and purple oozed onto the plate. I lifted the fork, blew on the pie to cool it a bit, and put the entire forkful into my mouth. OMG… it was a flavor explosion! It was absolutely the best pie, no, the best dessert, no, the best thing that I had ever tasted (sorry, Mom). I devoured the pie in seconds; and Martha served me another slice, which I gobbled down just as fast. Mitchell just watched me with a big smile on his face. He was taking his time, savoring the braslowberry heaven.

After we finished dessert, Mitchell stood up, wiped his mouth with the napkin that Martha put by his plate, and said, "We have had a long day, so I am going to show Daniel the guest room."

Martha stood up. "Of course, Mitchell. You two need to rest."

The cottage wasn't very big, and Mitchell walked me over to a doorway off the kitchen to the right. I looked in and saw two little beds that looked like they were built for toddlers.

"Do you have a preference?" he asked. I shook my head no. "Good," he said, "then I'll take this one," and he pointed to the one just inside the door. "It's closer to the bathroom, which is right there." Mitchell pointed to a closed door. "Why don't you get cleaned up?"

We took turns in the bathroom, then climbed into our respective beds. My feet were hanging off the end a bit, but once I got under the blanket and put my head on the pillow, I was out.

Chapter 13

I woke up to the wonderful smell of Martha's cooking. I sat up, rubbed my eyes, and looked over to Mitchell's bed. Mitchell was sitting on the edge of his bed, bending over and pulling on his boots. He looked up at me and said, "Oh good, you're awake. We should be leaving soon." He finished buckling his boots, hopped off his bed, and disappeared through the doorway. "Good morning, Martha." I heard him say with a little pep in his voice.

Martha answered, "Good morning, Mitchell. Did you sleep well?" He must've nodded because I didn't hear an answer. "That's good. I hope you two are hungry because I am making a big breakfast to fuel you up for your journey."

"Thanks, Martha. You are too sweet."

I slipped through the doorway just in time to witness Mitchell's bashful reply as he was looking down and blushing.

"Good morning, Daniel," Martha said as she noticed me walking through the doorway into the kitchen.

"Good morning, ma'am," I replied.

"Sit, sit, sit, you two," Martha said as she showed us to the table. There were freshly cut braslowberries in a big bowl in the middle of the table. Two plates were piled with food, some I recognized and some I didn't, and there was a fresh loaf of bread on the stove. Martha must've just pulled it out of the oven because it was still steaming. The teapot started to whistle, and Martha hustled over to turn it off. She brought it to the table and filled our empty cups.

"Dig in, Daniel!" Mitchell commanded with his mouth already full. I went straight for the braslowberries and put a big scoop on my already-full plate. Martha was in the corner of the room fussing with something I couldn't see. I quickly lost any interest in what she was doing when I took my first bite of food. Martha stood up, walked over to the stove, and sliced the fresh bread. She placed the sliced bread on another plate and set it next to the braslowberries.

"Thank you, Martha," Mitchell said.

I looked up and nodded and made an *umph* sound to express my gratitude.

Martha smiled at us both and returned to the corner of the room. It wasn't long before our bellies were full, our plates were clean, and our teacups were empty. "Thank you once again for everything that you have done for us, Martha, but it is time for us to go," Mitchell said with great gratitude in his voice.

"No need to thank me," she responded. Mitchell stood up, and I followed his lead. Martha shuffled over to us with her hands behind her back. "I have one more thing for you, Mitchell," she said. When she moved her hands from behind her back, she was holding a pointy blue hat with a big gold *M* in the middle. It was the spitting image of the hat the loloster had destroyed.

"Oh, Martha! It's perfect!" Mitchell exclaimed. "How did you…when did you…how…?"

"I started it last night when you went to bed, and I was able to finish it this morning."

Mitchell hugged Martha, and Martha hugged him back. When the embrace ended, there was a little awkward silence. "Thank you so much," Mitchell finally said. "This is the sweetest thing that anyone has ever done for me." Martha was smiling proudly from ear to ear. Mitchell pulled the hat onto his bald head and exclaimed, "Perfect!" There was a bit more silence, and then Mitchell finally spoke. His face was turned toward the ground; but he was looking at Martha when he asked, "Would it be okay if we stopped for a visit on our way back?"

"Of course," Martha said with compassion in her voice. She walked over and added, "I would be disappointed if you didn't." Then she kissed Mitchell on the cheek, and his face turned fifty shades of red as he made his way to the door.

"Thank you, Martha. We will see you soon." Out he walked. And I followed right behind him, but not before turning toward Martha and saying, "Thank you, ma'am. Everything was wonderful."

"You're welcome, Daniel. Take care of Mitchell for me," she responded. I nodded, turned, and out we went.

Chapter 14

Wanda was in my right hand as I jogged to catch up to Mitchell just as he was entering the woods on a dirt path. "Thank you, Martha. We will see you soon?" I laughingly teased Mitchell once I had reached him. "That's the best you got?"

"Shut up, Daniel!"

"Seriously, Mitchell. I'm ten years old, and I can do better than that!"

"Shut up, Daniel!"

"She stays up late to make you a hat. She kisses you on the cheek, and 'we will see you soon' is the best you can do? Sheez! It's no wonder you're single," I said jokingly.

Mitchell stopped, turned, and glared at me. Then he stuck his cane about an inch from my nose and stated, "For your information, I knew I might never get married when I agreed to go to work for King Salvatore. It is an honor to do so, and marriage often needs to be sacrificed in order to dedicate your life to the crown."

I felt bad. I knew I struck a chord. "I'm sorry, Mitchell. That is too bad. Martha is a wonderful person."

Mitchell kind of huffed as he turned away and continued walking. Under his breath, I heard him say, "She is more than wonderful. She is perfect."

We walked for a while in an uncomfortable silence until we started down a steep hill. "The end of the forest is at the bottom of the hill," Mitchell stated matter-of-factly. We carefully made our way to the base of the hill and passed by the final trees. As soon as we walked out of the woods, we were looking out over a large lake. The water was calm, and you could barely see the other side.

"Beautiful Lake Montville," Mitchell said with pride, "home of Junkita, the friendly sea monster. Well, friendly if you are good at heart. Somehow, she knows who is good and who is not." He looked me up and down. "Yeah, I think you'll be okay," he said, grinning.

"Sea monster?" I asked.

Mitchell chuckled under his breath and, ignoring my question, glanced to the right. "Come on, Daniel. This way." We walked about a hundred yards or so along the bank and came upon what looked like a row of wooden rafts. "This is how we cross."

We clumsily climbed across three rafts until we reached the one that had open water in front of it. The raft had three rings on top of three posts that passed down the middle of the vessel. There was a thick rope that went through each ring. The rope was attached to a tree behind us, and as far as I could tell, it traveled completely across the lake. Mitchell stepped to the front of the raft. "C'mon, Danny," he commanded. I carefully made my way to the front to join him. There was a little wiggle to the raft, but otherwise, I was surprised how stable it was. "Okay, Daniel, time to work some magic. Point Wanda at the rope in front of the boat and say 'pulleth.'"

I stepped up to the front and pointed Wanda at the rope about twenty feet ahead of the raft. I looked back at Mitchell, He nodded and flicked his wrist.

"Pulleth," I said with a flick of my wrist. A thin yellow light shot from Wanda's tip and traveled to the rope right where I pointed it. The light wrapped around the rope, became taut, and then yanked the raft forward. I stumbled back, and Mitchell actually fell back and landed with his feet straight up.

"Whoa," he said as he rolled into a seated position. "I think I'll ride the rest of the way down here," he said, laughing. "Keep going," he said with a smile.

"Pulleth, pulleth, pulleth," I commanded with bent knees, almost like I was surfing. I was able to keep my balance, and we made good progress. We were about halfway across the lake when the water started bubbling about twenty feet to the right of the raft.

"Stop!" Mitchell ordered.

We floated and watched the bubbles exploding at the surface like boiling water. Suddenly a bright-green figure appeared just under the surface. It was huge. I sat down, terrified of what might happen next, and then *whoosh*! A bright-green head popped out of the water. Its fire-red eyes stared at Mitchell and me. The creature's head reminded me of a *Tyrannosaurus rex*.

"That's Junkita," Mitchell whispered. The swimming dinosaur came closer. Her teeth were as long as my arm. As she breathed through her nose, water flew out her nostrils. She approached us slowly. Mitchell whispered again, "Stay still, Daniel." When Junkita reached the boat, she stretched her long neck and leveled her eyes at mine. She breathed heavily through her nose, and I felt the heat of her breath over my entire body. Then she cocked her head, looked up, and let out a giant growl. Fire roared from her mouth straight into the sky a hundred feet up. She looked back at me and opened her mouth. Her teeth seemed as sharp as razors. I sat there trying not to move, but I could feel my entire body trembling. Then, without warning, she looked down, stuck out her tongue, and, with one swipe, licked my entire body. She then looked at Mitchell, winked, and disappeared into the deep blue lake.

Mitchell began to roll around the raft in a fit of laughter. Meanwhile, I was dripping with the horrible-smelling saliva of the sea monster. "I love that Junkita," Mitchell said between his laughs. "What a sense of humor. Ha ha, what a card! Well, Danny, I guess she likes you!" I was speechless, still trying to comprehend what had just happened. "Okay, Daniel, that's enough messing around. Back to work," Mitchell ordered, still giggling.

I didn't even stand up. I just swiveled on my butt until I was facing the front of the raft. "Pulleth. Pulleth. Pulleth. Pulleth."

Before I knew it, we had approached the shore. With one empty raft between us and the land, Mitchell jumped up and moved past me to the front. "One more should do it," he said, and then jumped off the front of the boat onto the raft between us and the shoreline. "Come on, Danny." He held his hand out, but I jumped to the next boat without his help. I glared at him as I navigated past him to the land. I was still trying to process what had just taken place out there, and I wasn't happy that he hadn't warned me.

"There it is, Daniel," Mitchell said excitedly. I looked at him as he was pointing off into the distance with his cane. I looked where the cane was directing me and saw a distant castle on top of a hill. The castle was pretty far away, but it was easy to see that it was huge. There was nothing between us and the palace but rolling green pastures and a winding white stone road. "We are off to see the king!" Mitchell proclaimed. Then with the help of his walking stick, he headed directly toward the magnificent kingdom.

Chapter 15

As we approached the castle on the stone road, it became clear that the structure was more than just a castle—it was an entire city. The palace looked to be in the center of the metropolis, and it was majestic. "Welcome to Lordstown," Mitchell announced, "the capital of Annabellia!"

I was in awe. The place seemed to expand as we got closer. A wide moat, bordered by fifty-foot stone walls, appeared to encompass the entire city. A drawbridge—which had to be thirty feet wide and forty feet long—spanned the moat and was already deployed for easy access to the city. We crossed the drawbridge and entered an arched opening which must have been the main entrance into the capital. Two guards stood frozen at the gate, one on each side. The guards were much taller than we were. I'd say they were normal-sized adults, maybe six feet tall or just over. They were protected by armor from head to toe; but their face shields were open, revealing quite a surprise—bright-red skin. Not red like a sunburn, but red like shiny paint. Both guards stood at attention and held spears in front of them with both hands, the butt ends on the ground and the sharp tips toward the sky. They never looked at us, just stared straight ahead into the distance. Just as we were about to pass them…

"Welcome to Lordstown," they said in unison, still without looking at us. I jumped back, a little startled, and Mitchell giggled as we proceeded through the gate. There were throngs of people everywhere—all colors, shapes, and sizes. When I say all colors, I mean all colors. Some resembled Caucasians like myself and Mitchell. Others resembled African Americans, like the picture I saw of King Salvatore. I couldn't think of one human ethnicity that wasn't represented within my first thirty seconds inside this magnificent city. There were red people like the guards out front. There were people shorter than Mitchell and people taller than Shaq. The hair colors included every hue imaginable, and the styles were very big and elaborate. I mean like eighties style, if not even bigger and more poofy.

Most women—well, I guess every woman that I saw—wore extravagant dresses that were bright and sparkly. Most of the men were wearing what looked like suits—suits the color of Easter eggs. Some were solid, some striped, some plaid, but all were bold and bright. Many men were clean-shaven, but some had moustaches and goatees and beards. There were quite a few men and women wearing hats. Most of the women's hats were big and flowered, while the men's hats were flat and small, like the Irish cap my dad liked to wear, except, you know…bright.

Some people hustled around with a purpose, while others talked and laughed in groups. Scattered throughout the crowds, children in bright-colored shorts and suspenders played energetically. Scampering around them were, what I would say, pets of some sort—dogs but not exactly. The animals were medium-sized, bigger than poodles or pugs but smaller than labs or dalmatians. All of them were white and had a single little horn on their foreheads—like unicorn-dog hybrids. They were adorable, and they seemed to be having a blast playing with the children.

The entire city was constructed of stone and brick with quaint little stores dotting the streets. While there was little grass, elaborate pots and baskets of flowers decorated nearly every building. There were no cars or vehicles of any kind, so it seemed people just used the streets like sidewalks.

"Wow," I gasped, trying to take it all in.

"This way, Danny boy," Mitchell said as he gave me the old "come along" wave of his arm. He pointed to the castle which appeared to be the center of the city. "Time to meet the king." The palace wasn't far, and we arrived quickly.

As we approached the magnificent structure, I studied all the wonderful details of the palace. Multiple towers flew purple-and-gold Annabellian flags, which disappeared behind the giant gray walls as we got closer. Exterior stairways zigzagged from the ground up to the top of the walls, each leading to a closed wooden door. Dotting the walls were several glassless windows with wooden shutters, some open and some closed, but none were lower than fifteen feet off the ground. Lookout platforms were stationed every fifty feet or so with guards perched on each one. These guard stations were another ten feet above the walls, and it looked like they circled the entire city. However, despite the giant walls and the armored guards, the castle had a warm inviting feel to it. It's hard to explain, but I felt as though the city, as well as the palace, were inviting us in.

We entered through a massive wooden door in the front of the mansion. The room was huge and open. When I looked up, I could barely even see the ceiling. There were spiral staircases on both sides of the room that rose up several stories, and walkways with wooden doors lined the perimeter of each floor. The stonework of the walls and stairs was gray, but the railings looked like a white marble. I was still looking up when we were approached by an armored man with a spear. He was not wearing a helmet, and he was red like the guards near the front gate. His long black hair flowed past his shoulders. He lowered his spear parallel to the ground about waist high, not in a threatening way, but it was obvious that we were supposed to stop and listen to him.

"State your business, please," he commanded politely.

Mitchell puffed out his chest and, beaming with pride, said, "Mitchell Shrewsberry, to see the king!" He put one arm across his belly and the other behind his back and bowed. I cocked my head a little and looked at him. It was the first time that I had heard his last name. It was ironic to me because I went to school with a Brandon Shrewsberry, and he was the only kid in my class who was shorter than Mitchell. I shrugged my shoulders and thought it must be the name.

"And you?" the guard was looking at me now. He caught me off guard, and I began to stutter.

Mitchell spoke for me, "Daniel McGunny, also to see the king. He is expecting us."

"Wait right here," the guard ordered. Mitchell bowed again to show respect. The guard marched across the room to a giant double-doored entryway. Its huge red doors were trimmed with black iron hardware. The guard pushed open the twin doors, walked through, and disappeared behind them as they closed.

The guard wasn't gone for more than a couple of minutes when the doors flew open. Out ran a young boy who looked to be about my age. He was dark-brown-skinned like the king in the picture, and he was also bald like the king. "Mitchell!" he screamed as he ran toward us at full speed. The boy was wearing a long red fur coat that was open in the front and flowed like a cape behind him as he ran toward us and jumped up into Mitchell's arms. Mitchell caught him and, in one motion, spun in a circle.

"Prince Hugh!" Mitchell answered. "So nice to see you, but you're getting a little big for this."

"Awe, come on, Mitchell, I'm not that big."

Mitchell set the prince down. "Prince Hugh, I would like you to meet my dear friend, Daniel. Daniel, meet King Salvatore's son, Prince Hugh."

"Nice to meet you, Daniel," the prince stated as he stepped toward me and clasped his hands together, chest high.

"Thank you, and it is a pleasure to meet you, uh, sir?" I wasn't quite sure how to answer a prince, especially one that looked young enough to be in my class back home, but Mitchell was behind him looking at me and bowing. I quickly got the hint and gave the prince a bow.

"Mitchell Shrewsberry!" I heard a deep booming voice come from the big red doors. I looked up. It was the king. He was tall; I would say well over six feet. He was wearing the purple-and-white coat just like in the picture. The coat came down past his knees and covered up most of him; but he looked strong, athletic, and confident. He had the crown made from sticks on his head and a perfect smile upon his face. He was flanked by guards on each side wearing knee-high socks, white puffy knickerbockers, long-sleeved purple shirts, and they were holding spears. "It is always entertaining when you visit, but I am anxious to meet your friend."

"King Salvatore, may I present Daniel McGunny." Mitchell bowed, holding this bow while backing away, leaving me standing in front of the king by myself.

Prince Hugh ran behind the king and held onto his father's left leg while peeking around at me. "Daniel, we are excited, delighted, and grateful that you are here. Tommy needs our help, and he is our top priority. However, the conflict between Queen Kathelina and the good people of Annabellia has escalated. You see, Daniel, the queen has been here for generations, and until recently, we had always maintained friendly relations. There were occasions when the queen and past kings did not see eye to eye, but those disagreements never grew into serious disputes. Eventually, for whatever reason, the queen stopped visiting Lordstown. And she and her followers kept to themselves, well, for the most part. Lately, however, she has been aggressively antagonizing our soldiers, as well as the citizens of Annabellia.

"That brings us to Tommy Anderson. Tommy was tricked into serving under her for years—well, years in Annabellia. Rumor has it that he was asked to kill the prince." Prince Hugh buried his head into the leg of the king, and King Salvatore looked down and gently rubbed his child's head. He continued, "That is when Tommy finally figured out he was in bad company. So he decided to escape from the queen's court but made the mistake of confiding in Princess Gabriella. He couldn't have chosen a worse confidante. Gabriella, who many believe to be the mastermind behind the movement, immediately informed the queen. When Tommy attempted his escape, the queen herself caught him. He was tried, found guilty of treason, and punished severely. He has been a prisoner of the queen ever since.

"We have lost several brave men attempting to rescue him and return him to your world. You see, Daniel, the safety of human children has been and always will be of utmost importance to the kings and people of Annabellia." The King paused. "I'm sorry. Where are my manners? You two have traveled far. Shall we continue this discussion over a meal?" The king glanced back and forth between Mitchell and me. I looked to Mitchell for help in answering that not-very-hard question.

Mitchell spoke up, "Yes, Your Majesty. If it is not too much trouble, we would love a bite to eat."

"Follow me!" the king commanded. He turned and started toward the red doors. Prince Hugh never left his side, and the guards spun in unison and followed the king one step behind.

ANNABELLIA

Mitchell nodded at me, and we walked through the red doors side by side, a few paces behind the guards.

Chapter 16

We were led through the red doors into a vast perfectly square room whose floor was lined with beautiful square marble tiles. Within the tiles was a stunning mosaic that took up most of the room. It depicted a queen, dark-skinned like the king and prince, and she was wearing a golden gem-laden crown. The design and the colors were breathtaking. The room's ceiling was high and supported by thick wooden beams. Red and gold drapes, eight of them, met in the middle of the ceiling. The drapes alternated in color and were attached to the walls about ten feet above the ground. From there, the beautiful curtains hung straight down so that they were barely resting on the floor. White benches bordered the walls, but there was no other furniture in the room. We walked directly through the middle of the room to another set of doors. The king nodded at the two guards stationed on either side of the doors. They nodded back and opened the doors together.

Through the doors, we entered a spectacular dining hall. It was an enormously long, wide rectangle with sturdy wooden tables and strong wooden benches lining both sides. Each table could easily seat eight diners. Beyond the cluster of tables was a big empty space opening to a gigantic table that could probably seat fifty. Carved wooden chairs encircled the giant table.

Beyond the table was a series of broad marble steps in the shape of a semicircle that led to a marble platform. The structure reminded me of the altar at our church. A glittering gold throne backed by two towering wings sat proudly in the center of the platform. This impressive throne was flanked by two others—one identical to it but about half the size, and the other a bit smaller than the second.

Backlighting the thrones was a spectacular wall of stained glass which had to be fifty feet high. The vivid multicolored panels reminded me of an enormous kaleidoscope, and their intricate designs were almost hypnotic. I was spellbound. As a result, my eyes remained glued to the glass when *mmmmph, bam*, I walked right into the king's backside. I didn't realize he had stopped walking, and I banged into him so hard that I stumbled back a few steps. The king, on the other hand, didn't budge. Yet, as solid and athletic as the king looked, he felt oddly soft where I had bumped into him. It was weird.

"I'm sorry," I blurted out, afraid that I had just offended the king.

Mitchell looked down at the ground, sighed, and shook his head. He peeked up to see the king's reaction.

The king slowly turned his head, looked down, and smiled. "No need to apologize, Daniel. This room can be distracting." Prince Hugh giggled.

We had stopped in front of the huge dining table, and one of the guards pulled out the chair at the head for the king. The king's chair was much bigger than the rest and had armrests on it. The only other chair with armrests sat to the king's right. The other guard pulled out the chair to the left of the king, and Prince Hugh took his seat. One of the guards then motioned to the two chairs next to the prince's where we would be sitting. Mitchell sat next to Hugh, and I next to Mitchell.

The king picked up a bell that was on the table in front of him and rang it. Immediately, I heard a door behind me swing open, and then the shuffling of feet getting closer and closer. Before I knew it, there was an older woman standing right next to the king. She was dressed plainly, almost like a pilgrim, except her dress and bonnet were white.

"How may we serve you, Your Majesty?"

"Miss Elizabeth, my dear, I think we will have the VIP lunch feast today."

Hugh became visibly excited like he couldn't believe what he just heard.

"As you wish," the servant replied, then turned and was gone.

"I hope you boys have an appetite because you will certainly need it for this meal," the king said with a smile.

"Oh boy, oh boy, oh boy!" Prince Hugh exclaimed.

I had placed my wand on the table between Mitchell and me.

The king looked at me, nodded at the wand, and spoke, "Mitchell tells me you're a natural with that."

"I guess," I answered without much confidence.

"Did you name her?"

"Wanda," I answered.

"Ha ha!" the king belted out. "Wanda! Of course! Sounds like Mitchell's work."

Mitchell smiled proudly and shrugged his shoulders.

"So, Daniel, Mitchell tells me that you were born at 10:10 a.m. on ten-ten, or October 10."

"Yes, sir."

"Well, that explains your power. Nobody has entered Annabellia with those statistics in thousands of years, and it couldn't have come at a better time. We desperately need to rescue Tommy, but thus far, we have been unsuccessful on several attempts. The queen has thwarted all our efforts with relative ease, so we have reason to believe that she has become complacent and will not be expecting another attack anytime soon. So with your magic and our tactical planning, we believe we can catch the queen by surprise and safely rescue Tommy from her dungeon.

"With the help of Mitchell, I would like to train you and Wanda. We'll need to teach you a variety of spells, along with when and how to use them. Once we feel you are ready, we will put our plan into action. You see, as soon as Mitchell's bird, Christine, arrived with the news of your power, we started to devise a new plan. We intend to distract the queen with what she will think is an aerial attack. We have tried these before and failed. Hopefully, this will draw the queen and her army out of the castle, and you can then enter while she is gone. We have spies on the inside who know exactly where Tommy is. We will swoop in, free him, and return him safely back home before the queen even knows he is gone."

"What if she comes back before we are out?" I asked.

The king answered, "We don't foresee that occurring."

"Will you teach me how to defend myself and fight her just in case she does?" There was clearly some panic in my voice.

"Daniel," the king answered, "although you are potentially the most powerful human to enter our world in thousands of years, you are untrained, and your power pales in comparison to the queen's. You see, Daniel, you were born on ten-ten at 10:10 a.m., right?" I nodded. "Well, if someone was born at eleven eleven on eleven-eleven, they would be twice as powerful as you. Now, if someone was born on twelve-twelve at twelve twelve, then they would be twice as powerful as the eleven-eleven person. It is our belief that the queen was born on twelve-twelve at twelve twelve. Therefore, she would be four times as powerful as you, and she has been practicing magic for thousands of years. So you see, Daniel, it is imperative we remove her in order for our plan to succeed. Understand?"

That was a lot to digest, but I was pretty sure I understood. So I shook my head yes. Just then, the doors flung open behind us. I looked over my shoulder to see a small parade of servers entering in a single file line, carrying plates, glasses, and silverware. These were put in front of each of us, and an additional set was placed to the king's right. The servers then filled the glasses with a purple liquid.

I whispered to Mitchell, "Is this wine? I can't drink wine."

Mitchell laughed out loud. "Wine? No, Daniel, this is not wine. It's braslowberry juice." As the servers disappeared behind the swinging doors, I lifted my glass, smelled the juice, and sipped it—heaven!

As I was enjoying my second sip of braslowberry juice, the doors swung open again. This time, the servers, one for each of us, carried platters covered with silver lids, and they placed them on top of the empty plates in front of us. After putting down the platters, each server pulled out a dark-red cloth napkin, snapped it, and placed it on each of our laps. Oddly, there was a waiter also serving the empty chair, and I noticed that he even put a napkin on the vacant seat.

All the servers looked to the king. King Salvatore nodded, and in unison, the servers lifted the lids off our platters. They put the lids behind their backs, bowed, and walked backward, maintaining their bows for about ten steps. Then they stood up straight and walked out of the room in single file fashion.

I was overwhelmed by an incredible smell that redirected my attention back to my plate. The plate was almost overflowing. Dominating the platter was what appeared to be a small bird cooked to a golden brown. It was flanked by small white round balls and a dark-red pile of…I don't know…mush, I guess. Before I could ask, the king spoke, "Golden sandbernia!"

I had no idea what that meant, but I was pretty sure that he was announcing what I was about to eat. I looked down at the food, confused, and Mitchell whispered in my ear, "Chicken, potatoes, and applesauce."

"Ah," I said out loud, "it looks and smells wonderful. Will there be someone else joining us?" I continued, glancing at the empty chair.

I heard Mitchell sigh, and out of the corner of my eye, I saw him drop his head.

The king replied, "That place is for my wife, Queen Margaret. She will not be joining us, Daniel. You see, many years ago, she went out for a walk and didn't come home. We sent out a search party for her. It took us days, but we didn't give up. And we finally found her. She was near the edge of the stream below Dee Dee Bridge. She was alive, but she was in a deep sleep. She has been sleeping ever since here in her bed in the castle." I noticed a tear rolling down Prince Hugh's left cheek. The king continued, "We set a place for her at every meal because we know that one day, she will join us again."

"What happened?" I couldn't help it. I had to ask. If Mitchell's head could have sank any lower, it would have as he let out another sigh. "I'm sorry, King. I mean, Your Majesty, uh, sir."

"No, Daniel, it's fine. That is a fair question, and I can understand your curiosity." He took a breath and continued, "We knew she could not have survived a fall from the bridge, and besides, there were no signs of any injuries anywhere. We have reason to believe that Queen Kathelina put a spell on her—maybe even tried to kill her. Our spies have heard Queen Kathelina express her desire to be the queen of all of Annabellia. We also believe that Princess Gabriella had her hands in this tragedy as well. You see, our spies have informed us that Queen Kathelina has promised Princess Gabriella her castle if the queen overthrows us. As a result, it is our belief that Princess Gabriella has been behind the attacks against our people and that she has somehow come into possession of Tommy's wand. No native to Annabellia has ever been able to use a wand, but our spies say that

Gabriella seems to be making some progress possibly because she is a direct descendant of the queen herself."

"I want to kill both of them!" Prince Hugh belted out.

"Now, now, Hugh, first things first. We need to get Tommy Anderson safely home. Once Daniel and Tommy are safely back in their world and we are certain that no other humans are in Annabellia…that is when we will plan our attack. That is when we will avenge your mother."

"But we can use Daniel's powers to help us fight them and—"

The king cut him off. "Enough, Hugh! Daniel will not be a part of this war! He is doing more than we should have ever asked of him already. We need to get Tommy and get them both out of here!" The king lowered his voice and addressed us all, "Now, may we please enjoy this wonderful meal?"

I hadn't looked up since the king first raised his voice. I was moving the food around on my plate with my fork, but I did not feel comfortable being the first one to eat. So I waited. Finally, the king took a bite, and one by one, we followed. Not surprisingly, the food, again, was some of the best that I had ever tasted. That being said, I was unable to truly enjoy it since I was trying to digest the dialogue that I had just heard.

We finished the meal in silence. Mitchell was the last to clean his plate, and when he set his fork down, the king picked up and rang the bell. The doors flew open; and the servers came, cleared our plates, took our napkins, and placed a bowl in front of each of us. Each bowl contained a warm wet cloth. The king wiped his face with his cloth and returned it to his bowl. Everyone else followed suit; and the king broke the silence with, "Let us enjoy some dessert." He rang his bell again; and the servers immediately delivered small covered bowls, which they placed in front of us, and simultaneously lifted the lids. There was a steamy deliciously sweet-smelling pastry in the bowl. Prince Hugh had a bite in his mouth before the servers could even back away. Again, the food was phenomenal, and within minutes, there wasn't a morsel left in front of anyone.

"I hope you enjoyed your meals," the king said. "The guards will now show you to your quarters. Relax a bit and I will send for you shortly. Prince Hugh and I will then present the rescue plan and start your training." He raised his right arm and snapped his fingers. Two guards scurried from their posts at the door to the king's side. "Take them to the east wing guest room." The guards nodded to the king, and then nodded at Mitchell and me. Mitchell pushed his chair back from the table and stood up. I followed Mitchell's lead.

"Thank you for a wonderful lunch, Your Majesty," Mitchell said with a bow.

"Yes," I added, "it was delicious."

The king smiled at us both, and we followed the guards through a door to the right of the table.

Chapter 17

We walked down several stone hallways and past several doors. Each door was flanked by the familiar red-faced guards dressed in armor and holding spears. None of the guards made eye contact with any of us, but each one nodded at the escorts that we followed. Finally, we stopped at a double door; both guards each pushed open a door and, with a wave of their arms, silently invited us in. Mitchell entered first, and I was two steps behind him.

The room was enormous. It was bigger than my house. Okay, not really, but you get the drift. It had to be a hundred feet long and had thirty-foot ceilings. The walls were lined with small openings covered by bright-blue curtains. They resembled windows but had no glass. Along the walls were several shelves filled with pots of flowers and plants. At the far end of the room were two poster beds, one in each corner separated by about twenty feet and a square red-and-gold area rug. The posts of both beds were topped by red flags, and their tall mattresses were encircled by sheer-white drapes.

I slowly spun in a circle, marveling at the room. "Well, I guess we have to share a room," Mitchell said sarcastically with a chuckle. We approached the beds. I walked toward the one on our left, and Mitchell walked to our right. Near the head of each bed were small end tables holding teapots and cups. "Now this is service!" Mitchell exclaimed as he poured a cup of steaming tea. I lifted my teapot and did the same. With the teacup in my left hand and Wanda in my right, I brushed the bed's curtains aside using the wand. I took a seat on the softest bed that I had ever touched. I kicked my shoes off as I sank into the mattress and took a sip of the sweet-smelling tea. I didn't know why I was surprised, but I was delighted to find out it was braslowberry tea.

"Good tea, huh, Mitchell," I stated. I didn't get a response, so I glanced over to Mitchell's bed. He was lying on his back with his head on his pillow, which almost completely wrapped around his face. His hat was pulled over his eyes, and his hands were folded on his chest. His stomach was raising and lowering rhythmically, and I could hear him snoring. I set my half-empty teacup down and lay down myself.

"Ding! Ding! Ding!" Groggily, I sat up. I had absolutely no idea how long I had been asleep. At the far end of the room, standing at attention near the double doors was a guard. "Sir Mitchell and Sir Daniel." He was trying not to yell, but he knew his voice had to carry across the enormous room. He continued, "King Salvatore and Prince Hugh will be arriving shortly."

Mitchell sat up with his short legs dangling off the side of the bed. He rubbed his eyes and answered, "Thank you. We will be ready." The guard nodded, backed through the doors as he grabbed one with each hand, and continued backing up until we heard them close.

I jumped off my bed, bent over, and put on my shoes. I reached over and picked up Wanda, which I think I was holding throughout my nap, and I sat back down on the edge of the bed. Mitchell also pulled on his boots. He looked up at me, still sitting but with his knees bent and his arms wrapped around his legs. "This is going to be exciting," he said with a smile on his face.

"What are we going to do?" I asked cluelessly.

"I don't know the order. But I'm sure you will learn some magic, discuss the rescue plan, see the armies, and maybe even meet some officers."

Just then the doors sprung open. "I hope you two are well-rested." It was King Salvatore with Prince Hugh at his side. They approached us when Mitchell stood up and started to walk toward them. I followed closely behind. We were almost face to face with them when we all stopped walking.

"Well, son," King Salvatore addressed Prince Hugh, "do you think we can make a hero out of this fine young man?"

"I think we can, Dad," the prince answered eagerly.

Still looking at his son, the king asked, "What should we do first, Hugh?"

"Make him feel safe and start his training" was his answer.

The king rubbed Hugh's bald head. "You are absolutely right, my boy! One day you will make a fine king." King Salvatore looked at me. "We have a plan, Daniel, and your safety is our top priority," he said compassionately. "There may be some danger, but as important as it is to rescue Tommy, I do not want to risk the life of another human child to do it. If at any point I feel that the mission will not be successful, I will pull you out. Regardless, you will be home for your birthday dinner, Daniel."

I believed him, and I trusted him. Prince Hugh never took his eyes off me as his father spoke, and I knew I trusted him too. I looked the king in the eyes and replied, "Thank you, sir. I want to help Tommy. He deserves to be back with his family."

"Follow us," the king commanded with a smile. The father and son turned and started walking back to the doors that they entered through. Mitchell patted me on the back, both as a sign of pride as well as a push for me to follow the royals.

CHAPTER 18

Two guards, in armor, of course, led us out of the room. As we were walking through another stone hallway following the guards, the king began to speak, "We have two divisions in our army—a ground division, which is led by General McGill, and an aerial division that is led by me. I will have eyes on you throughout this mission, Daniel. Hugh will also be there to have eyes on me. You will be safe, and I am confident that Tommy will be rescued." As the king spoke, he looked straight ahead. He was all business.

I looked at Prince Hugh as he walked next to his father, puffing his chest out and beaming with pride. I was surprised to hear the young prince would be a part of the plan. But what did I know. Heck, I was only ten, and I was the center of this plan.

We started climbing stairs, a lot of stairs. The flights of steps went back and forth in straight lines, and we were surrounded by walls throughout our ascent. We finally reached a level platform with an open archway. "Guards!" the king barked, "Our cloaks!"

One guard circled behind the king, and one behind the prince. Simultaneously they lifted and removed the king's long purple cloak, as well as the prince's red one. What I saw next took my breath away. The two of them had wings—

giant wings that were folded against their bodies. They were light brown with some indistinct black specks and were white underneath. They reminded me of the colors of a hawk. The wings were broad at the shoulders and tapered down to points just above their calves. Both the king and prince flapped their wings a couple of times to puff them out. I dropped Wanda, and it clanged on the stone floor. Embarrassed, I quickly bent down and picked it up.

The king and Hugh proceeded through the archway, and Mitchell and I followed. We walked into what looked like a giant stadium without seats. It was shaped like an enormous oval, and I was pretty sure the walkway we were on traveled all the way around. There was a wooden rail in front of us, which also seemed to encompass the entire oval. As we approached the rail, the king exclaimed, "I give you the aerial army of Annabellia!"

I looked down hundreds of feet to the grass field below. There had to be a thousand soldiers lined up in perfect formation, all of them in red-and-gold uniforms with gold helmets. They all appeared to be dark-brown-skinned like the king and prince. We were high up, but some of the soldiers looked to be holding spears. Others held bows, and others had what appeared to be nets.

"Daniel, Mitchell." The king commanded our attention. "It is time for a demonstration! Hugh!" The king barked as he took about three steps toward the railing, and then dove over the rail and disappeared. Hugh ran after him and followed suit. I ran up to the wooden rail, grabbed on, and looked down. Just as I peeked over the edge—*whoosh*! The king soared inches from my face, straight up like a rocket. Prince Hugh was right behind him. They rose a hundred feet over our heads, made a couple of circles, and then dove down, leveling off about ten feet over the soldiers.

They started at the front of the pack and flew a complete lap around the army. As soon as they came to the right front corner, they shot straight up into the air. The soldier at that corner followed them up, and with almost no pause whatsoever, the others took off one by one. When the last soldier in the front row went up, he was followed by the soldier standing behind him. The army flew up one after another, row by row in a zigzag fashion. It reminded me of dominos being knocked over, except in reverse. Soon, the entire army was airborne, and soon after that, they were gone.

I was still looking up when I heard a commotion below. When I looked down, there were people everywhere, carrying what looked like mannequins and placing them all over the field. The mannequins were dressed like soldiers, and within minutes, there were at least five hundred mannequins spanning the field. At the far end of the field, a dozen or so workers wheeled out a cart, on top of which rose a giant wooden castle. It had to be four stories high.

The king's aerial army reappeared, and they hovered over the stadium while continuing to flap their wings. It was like they were treading water in the air. King Salvatore and the prince were in the middle of this swarm, and it was easy to see that the king was giving instructions. He blew into what I could only describe as a Viking's horn, then he and the prince flew up, and then turned sharply and flew away. The entire army followed, flying in the opposite direction of the wooden castle.

Within a few minutes, the field was clear of workers, leaving only the mannequins and the castle. I heard the horn again, and the king and prince shot over the top of the stadium like missiles. As soon as they passed us, they dove down. They sped toward the first line of mannequin soldiers and pulled straight up. Just then, a perfect line of about fifty soldiers came flying in. And about twenty feet behind them, another perfect line, and every twenty feet, another after that.

The first lines of soldiers all had spears. They swooped down, unloading their weapons at the mannequins, and shot back up, never breaking formation. The next group had bows and arrows, and they did the same. The targets were being obliterated. The third group had small cannonballs in nets. They wound their arms up, and then unloaded the weapons, nets and all. The soldiers were rapidly destroying the entire mannequin army. Line by line, the soldiers continued flying in and firing their weapons, and before long, not a single mannequin was left standing.

The horn blew, and the attack ceased. A group of about a hundred winged soldiers remained floating over our heads. The prince was in front, addressing them as the king looked over his shoulder. Prince Hugh blew into his horn; and the soldiers dispersed in every direction, then instantly shot into a formation of five lines with about twenty soldiers in each line. They were now all holding chains with some sort of ball at the ends. Their arms hung straight down so that the balls swayed about ten feet below them. Just then, they were joined by five more soldiers, all carrying flaming torches and lining up at the end of each row.

Prince Hugh gave his horn a short toot; and the torch-bearers flew under the formation, lighting each of the balls on fire. Five rows of bow-and-arrow-wielding soldiers merged into the formation and lined up above the fire carriers so that there was one soldier with a bow above every soldier with a flaming ball. Prince Hugh yelled something, and then raised his arm in a "let's go" motion.

The first set of soldiers descended in unison into the stadium and then straightened out about forty feet above the ground. The archers started shooting at the castle one arrow after another like they were protecting the flame-wielding soldiers. When the attackers reached about fifty yards out, they ceased firing. At about twenty yards, the flaming balls were launched all at once, and as soon as the flaming weapons were released, the soldiers shot straight up. The balls must have been soft because they acted like Molotov cocktails. As soon as they hit the castle, they exploded and ignited the entire structure. By the time the fifth line hit the castle, the wooden structure was an inferno. Mitchell and I just looked at each other in awe. The entire attack lasted less than two minutes, and the army took out five hundred soldiers and a castle.

Mitchell and I were staring down at the carnage when I heard, "Well, what do you think, Daniel?" I looked up and the king and prince were gently fluttering down. They landed softly right next to us.

"Wow" was all I could say.

"We are very well-trained, Daniel. You can see why I am confident in our troops, and I am confident in our plan to safely rescue Tommy and get you both home." The king continued, "Now that was just the aerial army. Let us go see the ground attack." King Salvatore and Prince Hugh folded their wings back into their bodies, and the guards draped the cloaks over their backs. "Follow me," the king commanded, and he and the prince proudly walked through the doorway a little taller after that perfect display.

Chapter 19

We walked down a couple of long hallways and came to another open archway. We could hear a lot of commotion as we approached the opening. On the other side of the arch was another arena, and again, we found ourselves looking down upon a rectangular grass field far below us. It was filled with soldiers in armor, engaged in battle. They all had shields, but some wielded swords. Some swung spiked balls on chains, and others flung spears. Even from a distance, you could hear the metal of their armor clanking. Soldiers were falling left and right.

Both ends of the field were lined with archers. Because they were not wearing armor, you could see they had the same bright-red skin of the castle-guards as did what appeared to be officers who were riding strange animals all along the perimeter of the battlefield. These mounted animals looked more like rhinos than horses. They had leathery gray-green skin and a horn at the end of their snouts. Their legs were thick and stumpy. The riders sat in saddles and held ropes that were attached to muzzles that covered the animals' mouths.

"Oh my!" I heard Mitchell gasp.

"Oh, don't worry, my friends," the king said, looking down at Mitchell. "This battle is not real. It is practice."

"It looks real to me," Mitchell argued. I didn't want to say anything, but I agreed with Mitchell.

"No, no, no, those weapons are not deadly." Just then the archers from the far end of the stadium launched hundreds of arrows high into the sky. The arrows flew over the soldiers who were battling and landed in another group of soldiers who were approaching the battlefield, dropping several of them to the ground. The king continued, "You see, the weapons are not sharp, and they all have colored markers on them. If a soldier gets marked with the other army's color, he is out of the battle, and he falls in place." The king pointed to the archers who had just fired their bows. "Do you see the blue bibs that they wear?" Mitchell and I both nodded. "Well, they are the blue team, and their bibs match the blue feathers on the helmets of their battle soldiers. The other team is yellow." I looked over the railing to see the archers below us in yellow bibs. "The marking color is like chalk. Those spiked balls are made of a heavy sponge, and the tips of the swords and spears and arrows are also spongy."

"Well, I feel better. Thanks, King!" Mitchell said with a sigh. Just then we heard a giant *whoosh*, and we saw a flurry of arrows soar into the sky from our end toward the blue army. Several soldiers from the blue army fell as the arrows rained down on them.

"Let us go down and meet the general." Led by the guards and with Prince Hugh at his side, the king walked back through the archway from which we entered. We descended several flights of stairs, finally arriving at what I presumed was the ground floor, and we made our way through a twenty-foot opening and walked right out onto the battlefield. The yellow archers were directly in front of us. The noise from the battle was deafening up close. It reminded me of a noisy factory, metal on metal with an occasional muffled yell from someone giving orders.

A man without armor approached us, riding one of those rhino-looking animals. "Whoa!" he commanded as he pulled back on the reins. The animal growled, snorted, and obeyed the order. The man then bowed to the king. "Your Majesty," he stated respectfully. He then bowed at the prince.

"General McGill," the king answered with a nod, "I would like to introduce you to Mitchell Shrewsberry and Daniel McGunny."

"Pleasure to meet you both, and I am looking forward to working with you, Daniel." He swung his right leg over the animal and dismounted gracefully right in front of us. He seemed a bit young to be a general, but what did I know? He had thick jet-black hair that covered his shoulders, and he had a very athletic build. He was wearing a short-sleeved shirt which showed off his muscles. He then held out his hand and nodded at us. Mitchell shook the general's hand, and I followed suit. I was studying the animal, and the general must've taken notice. "This is Boris," he said. "Boris is a mahoney. I don't believe you have those in your world." I shook my head, never taking my eyes off the magnificent creature. "Don't let the muzzle fool you, Daniel. He is friendly. You can pet him."

I walked up to the mahoney and rubbed his side. Boris let out a contented groan. He must have liked being petted.

"Wow," I said under my breath, trying to process what I was looking at.

"Your army looks ready, General." I heard the king say, distracting my attention from the friendly beast that I was rubbing.

"Yes, sir," the general answered confidently. "What is the time frame for Operation Rescue?" he asked.

"I have yet to work with Daniel, but based on what Mitchell has said, I think we can be ready in less than a week."

"Perfect, Your Majesty," he said with deep thought in his dark-brown eyes. "I will rest my troops after this evolution, and we will be ready and waiting for our orders."

"Carry on," the king stated, and with a nod, we were following him back out the stadium. "We will grab a bite to eat, and then your training will commence immediately after."

"Yes, sir," I answered as we followed the guards, the king, and the prince out of the building.

Chapter 20

We ate a light lunch, and then headed for the training facilities. As we made our way through the castle, the king informed us that the first few lessons would be outside but that eventually we would practice the rescue indoors. "We have created what we believe to be an exact replica of the dungeon where Tommy is being held," the king proclaimed. "We know where the nearest entrance is, what the best means of egress is, and where the guards will be stationed. But first, Daniel, we will practice here," the king said as we stopped at an open archway, and he motioned us through.

We walked onto an oval-shaped grass field with steep stone walls that rose straight up about fifty feet. The field was less than half the size of the other two fields where we had just watched the armies practice. Lined up along the far half of the wall about ten feet apart were mannequins dressed in armor. They were separated by a variety of objects halfway between each one. The objects included round targets made of hay, big round balls hanging from wooden structures, and piles of wood that looked like unlit campfires.

"Mitchell tells me your zaruna spell is pretty strong." The king looked at me and waited for an answer.

"Uh-huh" was my reply.

"Pick a pile of wood and start a fire, but be careful not to blow the wood away. You need to control your power." The king looked at me, and I nodded.

I took Wanda out of its sleeve and pointed to a pile of wood straight ahead of me. I flicked my right wrist and "Za!" I said it with very little enthusiasm. A small fireball shot out of Wanda's white tip, traveled about fifteen feet, fell harmlessly onto the ground, and burned out.

Out of the corner of my eye, I saw Mitchell slump in disappointment. "Don't worry, Daniel. You just need to figure out your distances along with the strength that you must use. That was the perfect fireball. Now you just need to gauge the distance. Try either 'za' with a little more umph or 'zaru' with a little less."

I looked at the same pile, flicked Wanda, and exclaimed, "Zaru!" The fireball shot directly where I was aiming, slamming into the woodpile and igniting it into an instant bonfire while only knocking off the top couple pieces of wood.

"Bravo!" the king exclaimed.

"All right, Daniel!" the prince shouted with excitement.

I looked at Mitchell, and he smiled proudly and nodded.

"Pick another woodpile and try that again," the king commanded. "Keep in mind that the next pile will be a little farther away."

I looked around, and I set my sight on another stack of firewood. "Zaru!" I said with authority and a flick of the wrist. The fireball left Wanda's white tip and sailed directly at my target. It hit dead center and lit the entire pile of wood on fire without knocking over a single piece of wood. Mitchell, the king, and the prince all applauded with a polite "golf" clap.

"Okay, Daniel, I am going to teach you a spell that I hope you will never have to use. It is only for dire circumstances. All the training that our armies have engaged in are specifically designed to help you avoid such circumstances."

The king paused, looked down, and said softly, "It is the death spell." He looked me in the eyes. I could also see the prince looking at me sheepishly, and when I looked at Mitchell, he was looking away. *This…stuff just got real*, I thought to myself. I looked back at the king and gave him an understanding nod.

"All right, Daniel, hold your wand straight out." I did as the king ordered. "Now, to perform this magic, the flow of your movements must be smooth. But first, we will practice in segments. With your arm straight out, point Wanda at the ground." I lowered my arm to about a forty-five-degree angle. "No, Daniel," the king corrected, "only bend at the wrist. Your arm must remain straight ahead of you." Again, I did as he said. "Now, with only your wrist, point the wand straight up." This time, I followed his directions correctly the first time. "Now snap your wrist down so that Wanda is pointing straight ahead of you." I did as he said. "Good, Daniel. Now try to do that all in one fluid motion." I held my arm straight, pointed down, swung the wand up, and snapped it straight ahead. "Very good, Daniel. Now pick out one of those knights against the wall and just as you are snapping toward him, yell, 'Killeth!'"

I set my eyes on a mannequin that was off to our left a bit. I pointed Wanda right at his chest. Down, up, "Killeth!" I said sternly and loudly.

Pfffff! I felt a little kick in Wanda, and an arrow shot out of its white tip with such velocity that there was not even a slight arc to its path. The arrow flew directly at the knight, and *pow*! It hit it dead center, obliterating the mannequin's armor. It was as if the arrow had an explosive tip at the end of it.

"Woah!" Prince Hugh said with amazement.

Mitchell rubbed his eyes to make sure he actually saw what had just happened.

"Nicely done," the king chimed in.

I took a couple of steps backward—excited, scared, and confused—while trying to comprehend the power that I had. For the first time, I realized that this power was not "fun" but rather dangerous. Wanda slipped out of my hand and fell to the ground. I had yet to take my eyes off the destruction for which I was responsible.

The king was aware of the apprehension that was coursing through my body. "Don't worry, Daniel." The king put his hand on my shoulder and looked straight into my eyes. "We will practice this spell. We will perfect this spell, but we truly do not plan on using this spell." He continued, seeming to look into my soul, waiting for me to acknowledge him. I nodded. "Very well," he said loudly as he took his hand off my shoulder. He bent over, picked up Wanda, and handed it back to me.

"Here's what I want you to do next." The king pointed at the knight on the far left. "One," he said. He then pointed at the knight on the far right saying, "Two," and then the one in the center. "Three. I want you to hit all three of those targets in succession. I want you to have all three shots off in about three seconds. Do you understand?" I nodded. "Okay then, whenever you are ready."

I took a deep breath, and then slowly exhaled. "Killeth! Killeth! Killeth!" I shouted as I fired at the three targets in the order that the king told me to. I hit the first one dead center, destroying the entire thing; the second, I hit in the right shoulder, knocking off his arm; and then the third, again I hit dead center. The noise of the exploding metal was deafening.

"Impressive," the king stated. "Now we are going to have a little fun." He looked down at me with a sly grin. "Hugh, go swing all the hanging balls."

"Okay, Dad," Hugh answered as he dropped his cloak to the floor, flew across the field, and began swinging the hanging balls. One, two, three, four in all.

"I want to make sure you can do this spell before we have a live trial." He clasped his hands together and rubbed them mischievously while he was looking at Mitchell.

"What are you up to, King?" a concerned Mitchell asked.

"Don't you worry about that, my good man" was his answer. The king then looked at me and said, "With your arm straight out and your wand pointing up, flick it at those moving targets and command them to 'freezeth.'"

I looked at the swinging ball that was farthest to the left, held my arm out and my wand up, and ordered, "Freezeth." A blue light shot out of the wand and hit the ball as it was swinging to the right, and the ball stopped right there like it was defying gravity. I then moved to the next one and the next and the fourth. "Freezeth, freezeth, freezeth." I hit all four and stopped each instantly.

The king then ordered, "Leave the first one alone because I want to see how long this spell lasts. But hit the next three with the same motion, using the word *free-eth*."

I did as the king instructed me, and one by one as a yellow light struck them, all three started moving in the same direction and at the same pace that they had been before they were frozen.

"Perfect. Now let's hit a moving target," the king said, chuckling as he looked at Mitchell.

"No!" Mitchell exclaimed, immediately guessing the king's intentions. "No, no, no, no, no!"

"Five…" The king began as he looked at Mitchell.

Mitchell crossed his arms and, in a huff, said, "No!"
"Four!" the king continued.
Mitchell took a couple of cautious steps.
"Three!"
Mitchell started running.
"Two, one! Get him!" the king commanded.
Mitchell was running in a zigzag pattern. I pointed my wand in his direction, and with a flick—"Freezeth!" The blue light shot directly at Mitchell, who was about twenty-five feet away. It hit him square in the back; and he came to an instant halt, statue-like. His right foot was planted on the ground; and he was leaning forward, defying the laws of physics. There was no way he shouldn't have fallen forward, but he didn't. I gasped and looked at the king. Prince Hugh was bending over crying-laughing with his hands on his knees.
"Ha ha!" the king roared. "A perfect shot, young Daniel! Now let's set him free!"
I quickly pointed Wanda at Mitchell. "Free-eth!" The yellow light struck Mitchell, and he instantly began running at full speed like he had never broken stride. He took about ten more steps, then slowed to a stop. He hunched over, out of breath, and complained, "Are you finished having fun?" He was barely able to get this out before he had to take another deep breath.
"You're a good sport, Mitchell!" the king belted out. "Come on back!"
Red faced and out of breath, Mitchell slowly walked back. Prince Hugh was still laughing. "Knock it off, kid!" Mitchell said with a chuckle, finally showing signs that he thought it may have been a little bit funny.

"What did it feel like?" I asked excitedly.

"It was weird. I knew I was frozen, but I didn't feel anything. I actually felt like I was still moving even though I could see that I wasn't."

"There it goes," the king stated as he pointed at the first ball which had just started swinging back and forth. "That took about five minutes. Good to know. That will be perfect to use on the guards who will be watching over Tommy. We will be long gone before they even know what hit them. That's enough for today. Guards!" Two red-faced guards were beckoned by the king. "Take our guests to their quarters so they can rest and clean up before dinner." The guards nodded at the king, and then nodded at Mitchell and me, instructing us to follow. We walked out of the arena behind the two guards and returned to our room.

Chapter 21

The next day, we practiced the zaruna, killeth, freezeth, and free-eth spells, and we ended the day by learning the protecteth spell. Just as Mitchell indicated on our journey to the castle, the protection spell was not an easy one. When I was able to perform it correctly, a light-green semi-visible circular force field would surround me. However, I was only able to get it right about twenty-five percent of the time. When I was able to raise the force field, the king, Hugh, and Mitchell would throw braslowberries at it, and the berries would spark and disappear. I kind of felt like a human bug zapper.

The king stressed that I needed to perfect this spell before we could attempt the rescue. It was different from the other spells because it was more than a flick of the wrist. I had to make a circle with my entire arm, and the circle had to start and end in the same spot or the force field would not be complete. And it would break apart and fizzle out. The other difficulty of the protection spell was that it was physically demanding. All the other spells were a flick of the wrist. With this one, I had to concentrate and hold the spell. It was as if I had something pushing back against me every time a braslowberry hit the shield. I felt like I was getting punched in the arm. Sometimes the berries would knock out the force field completely.

Over the next few days, I mastered the first four spells, and I was becoming more proficient at the protection spell. I was able to get the force field up every time, and I was repelling rocks instead of braslowberries. I even started practicing the spell with Mitchell and Prince Hugh inside the force field with me. The king said that he had never seen a three-person force field performed before. Not only was I able to do it, but I believed I could fit even more people within the shield. Once the king was convinced that I had complete control of the spell, he determined that it was time for a true test. "This," he said, "is going to be interesting."

The next day, the king called Mitchell and me to the practice field first thing in the morning. There were two armored mannequins set up in the middle of the field about five feet apart from each other. About twenty archers circled the mannequins. The king stood with Prince Hugh at his side as we walked in.

"Okay, Daniel." The king pointed at the lifeless armored guards. "I want you to get between those two and create a force field. The archers will then shoot flaming arrows at the armored guards. They will not be aiming at you, so don't worry." I looked at Mitchell, and then I looked back at King Salvatore. "Don't worry, son." He assured me. "Everything will be all right." Hesitantly, I headed toward the middle of the field.

When I reached the two mannequins, I heard the king yell, "Archers! At your ready!"

The archers drew back on their bows, and then dipped the tips of their arrows in small flaming bowls that flanked each one. They then aimed their weapons in my direction.

"Protecteth!" I screamed as I waved my arm in a circular motion, summoning my light-green force field. The force field was buzzing. I had never heard that before, but since I was so scared, I think this may have been my strongest effort yet.

"Aim!" the king yelled.

"Fire!" Prince Hugh finished the command.

Twenty flaming arrows simultaneously rained down on my force field. *Zap, zap, zap.* The arrows disappeared as they hit, and I felt like I was being gut-punched with each zap. After just a few seconds, I ended up on my butt. I saw the force field had disappeared, and I was winded. But when I looked to my left, I could see that the guard was untouched. Unfortunately, looking to my right, I could see a single arrow sticking out of the mannequin's armor directly in the middle of his chest.

The king, the prince, and Mitchell rushed toward me. "Are you okay, Daniel?" Mitchell yelled as they approached. I was sitting with my knees bent and my arms around my legs, still holding Wanda with my right hand. I looked up and nodded. Prince Hugh was the first to reach me, and he held out his hand to help me up. I grabbed it, and he pulled me to my feet.

"That'll be all!" the king yelled as he motioned toward the archers. They lined up and walked out through the archway two by two. "Well, Daniel, I am very impressed," the king stated. "But you still have a ways to go."

We took a break, and then came back and practiced the rest of the day. We continued practicing for the next two days. With time and constant practice, my force field was actually becoming brighter and less transparent. The king informed me that this revealed strength. "You will always be able to see out of your force field. But the harder it is to see in it from the outside, the stronger it is. Tomorrow, we will bring the archers back."

Chapter 22

The next morning, breakfast was brought to our room, and the servant informed us that the king would be summoning us soon. We enjoyed some pastries, tea, and of course, braslowberry juice. The king knew how much I enjoyed that drink, and he made sure that it was served at every meal. It wasn't long before the guards called upon us to follow them to the practice field.

We entered through the archway and walked into the small stadium. This time, there were closer to a hundred archers. They stood up against the wall, and they lined the entire circumference of the oval. Two armored mannequins were, again, placed in the middle of the field, but this time they were about ten feet apart. The king and the prince were waiting for us inside. "How are you feeling today?" the king bellowed.

"Very good, Your Majesty," I replied.

"Outstanding! Put this on and follow me, Daniel." He handed me a coat of armor and a helmet. The armor was a shiny silver, and the helmet was topped with a red feather. It was just a coat and helmet—no pants. But I figured the king knew what he was doing, so I didn't question it. With Mitchell's help, I put on the bulky armor. Then as the king walked toward the middle of the field, I followed closely, albeit clumsily, in my armor. We reached the two lifeless armored guards when the king turned and faced Mitchell and Prince Hugh. King Salvatore looked down at me and said, "You will protect all four of us today." I looked up at him with concern and shock. "Don't worry, Daniel," he said soothingly. "I know you can do it. I trust you."

Just then, he motioned toward Prince Hugh. The prince stood tall and shouted, "Archers! Round 1 at your ready!" About one out of every ten archers stepped forward and drew their bows. They were equally spaced and surrounded us in every direction.

The king looked down at me and closed my face shield. "You ready?" he asked.

"Fire!" the prince yelled before I could answer the king. Arrows flew right at us from every direction. The soldiers had aimed high and arched the arrows. But they were all right on target—and that target was us. I dropped to one knee, held Wanda over my head, and…"Protecteth!" I screamed. I felt the shield blast out of Wanda's tip as the pressure pushed back against me. I looked to my left, and then my right. I had successfully generated a shield big enough to cover the four of us. The force field was a perfect dome, which extended about ten feet up directly above the king and me, and it reached the ground all the way around the four of us. *Pfft, pfft, pfft.* I heard the arrows disintegrate against my bright-green shield.

"Ha ha!" the king bellowed. I still had the shield up. "You can release it now," the king instructed. So I flicked my wrist, and the green curtain seemed to be sucked right back into the wand. There was a bit of a kick right at the end, and it almost knocked me over.

"Nice work, Daniel!" the king congratulated me. "You held that shield with strength for a solid ten seconds. That is not an easy feat. How did it feel?"

"It felt good, Your Majesty," I answered with pride.

"Okay, Daniel, this time I want you to try something different." I looked up at him for instruction. He continued, "I want you to hold the shield in front of us. I don't want it touching the ground. You see, if you can keep the shield in front of you, then you can move with your shield deployed. Understand?" I nodded. "Okay, now hold Wanda straight out and form your shield."

I held the wand out. "Protecteth!" I commanded, and a circling green shield came into shape in front of me. The green light was still attached to Wanda's tip, and it looked as though the wand was continuously feeding the protective sphere. The shield wasn't very big, maybe about the size of a garbage can lid. The force was pushing against me, but it wasn't very strong. And I had no problem keeping my balance.

"Now move your wrist in circles, Daniel, and the shield will grow." I did as the king said, and with every completed circle I made with Wanda, the spinning shield grew. I kept going until the circle was protecting both me and the king. "Now," said the king, "let's slowly turn in a circle, and whatever you do, do not lose your concentration." We started rotating, and I managed to keep the shield up. We turned halfway around so that we were facing Mitchell and the prince.

"Archers!" I heard the prince yell. "Fire!" The archer directly to the prince's left fired, and then the next and the next. The shots were separated by a second at most.

"Protect, Daniel!" the king belted out. One by one the arrows disappeared into my bright-green spinning shield. We continued our slow revolution, keeping the most recent shooter directly in front of us. We were about halfway around when I started getting tired. The shield was losing color, and my arm felt like spaghetti. "Daniel!" the king shouted. "Do not lose this shield!" I sucked it up. The color returned, and the shield grew stronger. The next thing I knew, we were looking at Prince Hugh again. "That a boy!" King Salvatore said with pride. He looked at Prince Hugh and nodded.

"Fire!" Prince Hugh yelled. At this command, all one hundred archers shot their arrows simultaneously up in the air and toward us. I looked up, and the arrows had reached their peaks and were heading back down directly upon us.

"Protect us all, Daniel!" the king ordered.

Again, I dropped to one knee and pointed Wanda straight up. "Protecteth!" And a bright-green dome formed over us. I glanced down and could see that the two mannequins, as well as the king and myself, were completely surrounded by green. Just then, I heard all the arrows hitting the shield. It sounded like we were sitting in a car during a hailstorm, and with every hit, I became a little weaker. The attack was over in seconds, and most of the color from the shield had diminished. When I flicked my wrist, the shield completely disappeared. The king looked down and patted the top of my helmet.

Squawk! I heard and looked up to the sky. There was a huge bird circling the small stadium a couple of hundred feet up. It was bright blue, and I could see that he had a giant yellow beak. The king held out his right arm, and the bird instantly went into a dive headed right for us. The bird swooped down and, with a couple flaps of its enormous wings, almost stopped in midair. It softly landed on the king's outstretched arm, its talons completely circling the king's forearm. Around the bird's neck was a rope holding a small container.

With his left hand, the king plucked the container from the rope. He then shook his arm, and the bird dismounted and glided to the ground where it began pecking at the grass. From the container, the king pulled out a rolled-up note. He straightened the paper and read the letter. "Oh dear," he gasped. He looked at Hugh, Mitchell, and me, now all gathered at his side. "We are running out of time. We have to set out tomorrow. Princess Gabriella intends to execute Tommy in four days." The king looked right into my eyes. "We will practice the dungeon rescue this afternoon and head out at first light tomorrow. Now go grab a bite to eat, and the guards will bring you to the practice dungeon in one hour." Silently, we all acknowledged the king. Mitchell and I then followed the guards back to our room where lunch was waiting for us.

Chapter 23

The walk to the dungeon was much longer than the earlier one to the stadium. We finally descended two flights of stairs where the king and prince were waiting for us. "Daniel, Mitchell," the king acknowledged our entrance. We both nodded. There was an uncomfortable aura in the air this time. For the first time, I could see obvious signs of distress on the king's face; and the prince was not smiling, which also made me uncomfortable. "Daniel, I have to be honest with you. I was planning on more practice, but I do feel as though you are ready." I looked at him, trying to read his level of concern. "We have altered the plan, and to help ensure your safety, I will be with you for the rescue. I will lead my air attack, and then I will leave them and meet up with you." I nodded my head, letting him know that I understood.

"Then I too shall be with Daniel!" Mitchell demanded.

The king looked at him, thought for a second, and replied, "Very well." Mitchell nodded proudly. "All right, gentlemen, this is what we believe the dungeon will look like." The king led us through a stone archway. Again, we were above the site looking down. Below us loomed a dark room with a dirt floor. Through the gloom, we could make out seven mannequins shackled to the wall about twenty feet apart. The king pointed at them. "We believe there to be seven prisoners right now, and Tommy will be the one in the middle. I looked at the prisoner in the center and realized that it wasn't a mannequin but was a real person. "Daniel, this is important." I looked at the king. "You won't recognize Tommy because he will look like an old man." Again, I nodded. "You will have to make sure that it is him. Regretfully, we cannot worry about the other six. We will be pressed for time, and Tommy will not be able to move very quickly. Our timing is also important since the prisoners are taken outside twice a day. When they are outside, there are no less than ten guards watching over them. However, when they are shackled in the dungeon, there are just two.

"The aerial attack will be a diversion. The queen's army will think that we will be the ones attempting to free the prisoners, but in actuality, we will be drawing their forces away from the dungeon. When we pass over the castle, we will fire weapons to simulate an attack. Once we pass over the castle, I will peel off and meet you at the opposite side. I will have two other soldiers with me, and we will lift you and Mitchell over the wall and drop you near the dungeon entrance. You will enter there, freeze the two guards, and release Tommy. You will then meet us at the same spot where we first dropped you, and we will lift all of you back over the wall. At that point, the two soldiers and I will return to and rejoin the air forces while the three of you will head to the open field that leads to the woods.

"Our ground forces, led by General McGill, will be stationed just outside the woods. You will pass through the army, and they will prevent any enemy guards or soldiers from stopping or following you. I will give you a map which will guide you through the woods to a safe place to spend the night. Based on Tommy's health, I don't expect you to get there very long before dusk. The next day, you will follow the map back to Lake Montville, and from there, Mitchell will be able to get you home. You will cross Lake Montville and return to the mountains of Magnolia. It will still be daylight, so the lolosters should not be very active. You will continue back toward Mitchell's home and should get to your gateway in just a few hours. Make sure that you and Tommy are both holding on to Wanda when you twist it in your gateway keyhole. You must both be in contact with the wand in order to return to your neighborhood." I looked at Mitchell, and we both turned toward King Salvatore. "I know that is a lot to process, but we don't have that much time. Do you have any questions?"

"Yes, King," I answered, "I'm confused by one thing. After I free Tommy from the dungeon, why can't you and your soldiers just fly us all the way back to the gateway? Wouldn't that be faster and safer?"

"I wish we could, Daniel, but unlike ants, we cannot carry heavy loads for long periods of time. Even the strongest of soldiers can carry extra weight only for very short distances. The strain that heavy loads put on our wings not only can drop us from the sky but can also cause irreversible damage, rendering us flightless—that is, if we survive the fall."

I gave the king an understanding nod, and we walked through a corridor and back outside. "Here is where we will drop you off after we have lifted you over the wall," the king instructed. "We will remain out here to watch for any signs of trouble. The whole escape should take less than five minutes, Daniel. It is simple. First, freeze the guards, and then release Tommy's shackles by flipping your wand upward and commanding, 'free-eth.' Got it?" I nodded. "Keep in mind that you will have to do one 'free-eth' spell for each cuff. There may be two, or there may be four. But either way, you can fire them rapidly. Our 'prisoner' today has on four shackles. You should be able to freeze the guards before they know you're there, but even if they see you, they will be helpless against your freezeth spell. Are you ready to try this?"

"Yes, Your Majesty," I answered.

"All right. One, two, three, go!" He kind of caught me off guard, but Mitchell and I scurried down the first hallway and came to a low archway. I stopped and motioned for Mitchell to stop behind me. I peeked through the archway and saw the entrance to the dungeon, which was flanked by two armored mannequins. I pointed with my wand and shouted, "Freezeth! Freezeth!" Wanda zapped both of them.

We rushed past the frozen guards, hurried down some steps to the dirt floor, and ran to the prisoner in the middle. I quickly declared, "Free-eth! Free-eth! Free-eth! Free-eth!" With my commands, four little blue streaks hit each shackle, and the man was instantly uncuffed. He pretended to be old and helpless, so Mitchell and I helped him to his feet and led him out of the prison. We made it outside, and we were lifted over the wall by the king and two soldiers. After being gently dropped on the ground, we ran across a field, dragging the fake Tommy until we reached the woods.

"Six minutes and twelve seconds!" shouted Prince Hugh.

"Not bad at all," said the king. "I would like to see you knock off another minute from that time. Let's try it again. But this time, as you get past those guards on your way out, freeze them again."

"Yes, Your Majesty," I answered.

We practiced it again…and again and again and again. By the last time, we had it down to four minutes and twenty-two seconds.

Finally, the king said, "That is sufficient. Now let's get some food and some rest. We will be leaving at first light. We will have Tommy in our possession the day after tomorrow, and he will be home in three days!"

Wow! I thought, *three days*. But then it hit me. While all of this was taking place, my brother and his friends were still playing baseball. It was still my birthday, and I was still going to be home in time for dinner!

Chapter 24

The next morning, two guards woke us up. It was still dark out. "The king requires your presence for breakfast," they informed us. I sat up, rubbed my eyes, and looked at Mitchell. Two servants followed the guards into our room. One offered me a glass of braslowberry juice, which I quickly finished, while the other held a bowl out to Mitchell.

Mitchell answered the guards, "Very well. We will be ready in five minutes." He then looked at me and eagerly declared, "Let's go, Danny boy!" He jumped out of bed, looked in the bowl, and pulled out a washcloth. He wiped his face with the warm wet towel that the servant offered him, and then returned it to the bowl with a thankful smile and nod.

When we arrived for breakfast, we found King Salvatore, Prince Hugh, General McGill, and another winged soldier already seated at the table. They all stood as we entered the room.

"Daniel, Mitchell, I would like you to meet Colonel Timothy Joseph. The colonel is second-in-command in our aerial army. He will be in charge of the air troops when I peel off to help you over the wall." The colonel nodded at us. He was a very athletic-looking man who looked to be around forty years old. Like the king and prince, and the rest of the aerial army for that matter, he had dark-brown skin and no hair. "Please sit," the king said as he took a seat himself. We all followed his lead and were soon flooded by servants bringing us all kinds of food. I did not eat very much, probably because I was nervous and did not know exactly what to expect over the next couple of days.

I sat silently and picked at my food while listening to the small talk between the king, general, and colonel. After a few minutes, the king stood and declared, "We will begin our trek immediately after breakfast." He looked at Mitchell and me and continued, "We have armor for both of you which will be transported by our soldiers during our journey. Once we approach the queen's castle tomorrow, we will have you put it on. I suspect that it will be unnecessary. Regardless, we want you to don it as a precaution." Mitchell and I both gave understanding nods to the king. "The ground army will lead the journey followed by the four of us." The king pointed at himself, Prince Hugh, Mitchell, and me. "The aerial army will be behind us. I don't anticipate any dangers today. There is an elevated pasture about one hour from the queen's castle. We should reach that at dusk. From there, we will be able to see for several miles in every direction, and we will have guards posted all night long. At first light tomorrow, we will perform our rescue. General McGill, will you explain the procedures for tomorrow morning?"

The general stood up and replied, "Of course, Your Majesty." He looked at us. "Daniel, my ground forces will lead you to the edge of the woods outside the castle. The air troops will be following us. Therefore, you will have an army in front of the two of you and an army behind you both. When we reach the edge of the forest, we will signal the air troops. They will then fly over the castle, simulating an attack and drawing the queen's forces out to the far side of the complex away from Tommy. Just as the aerial attack commences, we will usher the two of you to the front of our army. There, we will wait for the king and his two soldiers to return. As they approach, you and Mitchell will run for the near wall. I will be able to show you exactly where to go. You will be lifted over the wall. Head to the dungeon, freeze the guards, and free Tommy. You will then lead Tommy back outside where the king and his men will be waiting for you. You will be lifted back over the wall, and return to the woods where the ground army will be waiting to protect you from anyone who might follow. We will guide you safely into the woods, and you will then follow the map to the secret cave. After spending the night there, you will leave at first light the following day. From there, you will proceed to your gateway and take Tommy home."

The general held out the map, and Mitchell grabbed it. He traced a line with his finger to the cave. "Mm-hmm," he said. He then traced a line from the cave, across Lake Montville, and back to my gateway. "Okay, seems simple enough." He looked at me. "I got this, Daniel. No worries."

We finished breakfast and headed out. Just as the king said, it was a very uneventful trip. We didn't talk much, and when someone did say something to me, I either just nodded or gave a one-word answer. As I considered the enormous size of the king's armies, I was wondering if this was overkill or if the whole thing was going to be a lot more dangerous than anyone was letting on.

We traveled through forests and pastures and valleys and more forests. Eventually, we began an ascent up a winding dirt path through some woods until we reached a wide open area. We continued climbing and climbing through this treeless expanse. My legs were getting sore; and poor Mitchell was beet-red with exhaustion, using his walking stick with every step. Finally, the ground leveled out to a giant circle-shaped plateau. Without a word, the soldiers from both armies went to work. They put up tent after tent. A larger tent was set up right in the middle of this sea of smaller ones. The soldiers then prepared campfires every twenty or thirty feet. I was impressed. This barren plateau had been transformed from an open field into a temporary community in a matter of minutes.

The king called for Mitchell and me, and we followed him and the prince into the center tent. "Your humble abode," he said as he waved his arm to show us our beds. "The cook is preparing dinner, and it will be brought in here. May I suggest an early night? We have traveled far today, and the next couple of days will be physically demanding." Mitchell and I nodded in agreement at the king. "Very well, I will leave you two to rest. Our tent is the one right outside your door." The king bowed toward us as he backed through the doorway and disappeared outside.

Dinner was brought to us after just a few minutes. Mitchell destroyed his dinner as I merely picked at my food again. "Are you okay, Daniel?" Mitchell asked.

"Tell me we're gonna be fine," I responded with a whimper, barely holding back my tears.

"King Salvatore would never let anything happen to you" was his answer. I ate a little more, crawled into my makeshift bed, pulled up the covers, and rolled so I was facing away from Mitchell. I stared at the cloth of the tent without moving for what seemed like hours. Finally, exhaustion overtook my body, and I faded off to sleep.

Chapter 25

I awoke the next morning to a commotion outside our tent. I sat up and rubbed my eyes. I looked over at Mitchell's cot, it was empty. I stood up and made my way to the tent door, and when I looked out, I saw the soldiers dismantling the camp just as quickly as they had put it up.

"Good morning, Daniel," I heard from my left. I looked and saw King Salvatore smiling at me. Prince Hugh, General McGill, and Mitchell were standing with him. "It is going to be a good day," the king said as he rubbed Prince Hugh's head. I stepped out of the tent and made my way toward the four of them. The king raised his right hand and snapped his fingers. "How about some braslowberry juice for our hero?" A soldier appeared from nowhere carrying a pitcher and a tray of glasses. He handed me an empty glass, and then filled it with a smile.

"Thank you," I said, still foggy from my slumber. The soldier nodded, bowed, and backed away with a smile on his face.

"Today is the day that Annabellia returns to normalcy!" the king proclaimed. "Let us have a bite to eat, and then be on our way." We made our way to a campfire and sat on the ground. A small group of soldiers brought us breakfast served on flat stones with no silverware. The king smiled at me and picked a bite of food up with his right hand and shoved it into his mouth. The others followed suit, and I did as well. Of course, the food was delicious. But I still didn't have much of an appetite, so I only had a few bites.

During breakfast, we discussed the plan again, and the king's confidence in the whole ordeal was soothing. For the first time, I truly believed that this might not be so bad. We finished eating, and the king ordered General McGill to gather the troops. He summoned a soldier who immediately scurried off. A bugle or some kind of horn sounded, and the soldiers started moving in every direction. The general wished us all luck, and then disappeared into the organized chaos of his army. Within a minute or two, the soldiers were lined up in perfect formation.

Prince Hugh had disappeared during the raucous proceedings but soon returned carrying two sets of armor. "Here you go, boys," he said with a smile as he handed us our gear. We slipped it on and stood on either side of the king. Two guards appeared, each one carrying a flag of Annabellia which was purple and gold with a winged coat of arms in the middle. We all lined up next to the king. On the king's left stood Prince Hugh and a flag-wielding soldier. On his right were me, Mitchell, and the other flag-carrying guard. The king drew his sword, raised it over his head, and roared, "Onward march!"

The ground army led the way, followed by us with the aerial army trailing. We marched down the plateau into the woods, then silently followed a trail through the forest. The armor I was wearing was not light but not too heavy either. The march was a pretty short one, and before I knew it, the entire army had halted. I looked forward, but I couldn't see over the tall soldiers who were in front of me. Soon, the soldiers opened a path down the middle of the formation, and General McGill walked out of it. "We are here," he said looking at the king. He continued, "It is time."

The king acknowledged the general and patted the top of my helmet. "Let's go get Tommy," he said. We walked through the path of soldiers who were standing at attention with the butt of their spears on the ground and the blades pointing straight up. Each one nodded at us out of respect as we walked by them. Once we reached the front line, we were at the edge of the forest looking out across a large green pasture and a giant gray castle.

General McGill spoke, "The wall straight ahead is the one we need to go over." I looked at where he was pointing and saw a part of the wall that was much shorter than the rest. This portion was probably about ten feet high and about twenty feet long. The wall went up another ten feet on both sides of this shorter section. McGill continued, "Once you are over the wall, take the corridor to the right. When you come to the first doorway, you should see the prison guards. There should be only two. Freeze them, free Tommy, refreeze the guards on the way out, and meet the king and his men right by the wall where they dropped you. My army will be waiting right here to give you safe passage back into the forest."

"Can I come, Dad?" Prince Hugh piped in.

"Yes, son. It never hurts to have an extra set of eyes on the operation. Besides, it will be good practice for when you are king one day." Two aerial soldiers appeared next to the king. "This is Sergeant William Bernard and Private James Edwards. They will be assisting you over the wall." They nodded at us, and we nodded back.

"All right!" the prince exclaimed excitedly.

The king then turned to Mitchell and me asking, "Are you ready?" We both nodded. "Very well. Let us begin." I looked at Mitchell, and he winked at me. I drew Wanda from its sleeve as we stepped out of the forest onto the green grass.

Chapter 26

We were standing at the edge of the tree line when the king took three steps and leaped into the air. Suddenly, with a *whoosh*, the aerial army came soaring over our heads, following the king, and headed directly for the castle. The first several lines of flying soldiers were armed with flaming balls and were followed by archers, and then soldiers wielding two spears each. As they approached the castle, they took a ninety-degree turn and headed straight up. They leveled out about fifty feet above the castle, and when they were directly over the center, the soldiers in the front released their flaming weapons. Just as the first bomb landed, a loud bell started ringing to signal the attack. The soldiers then flew to the far side of the castle, pulled an about-face, and came to a floating stop as the archers flew past them and lined up behind them. The soldiers armed with two spears flew next, and as they passed the first line, they each tossed one of their spears to a soldier who dropped a bomb. The entire army was armed again, but I soon saw enemy arrows flying up at the aerial army as the bell continued to toll.

"Now!" Sergeant Bernard barked at us. We immediately headed toward the access point at the pace of a slow run or a fast jog. I never took my eyes off the aerial army until the building blocked my view as we got close. Prince

Hugh, Sergeant Bernard, and Private Edwards flew directly over our heads about ten feet above us. Just as we were approaching the wall, the king flew over us in the opposite direction and shouted, "Fall out!" Private Edwards and Sergeant Bernard peeled off and disappeared behind us. Within seconds, I felt my feet leave the ground, and I looked to my right. Sergeant Bernard had wrapped his arms and legs around Mitchell and was flying him over the wall. I tilted my head back and saw that the king was doing the same for me. In seconds, we were over the wall and placed softly back on the ground. "To the right," whispered the king. "We will be right here waiting for you." I looked at the king and nodded.

Mitchell and I entered the castle and crept down a long hall. Mitchell was in front of me, and when we approached an archway, he held his arm out to stop me. I stood motionless for a few seconds, and then he waved his hand for me to approach him. When I reached him, he whispered, "Freezeth." He then gestured for me to come around him. I did so and peeked around the corner, I saw two guards. I pointed Wanda at the one on the left.

"Freezeth!" The light shot from Wanda's tip and hit the guard square in the chest before he had any idea what was happening. The second guard swung his head around, but before he could draw his sword, I yelled, "Freezeth!" Just like that, we had easy passage into the dungeon. We passed the frozen guards and looked below us. Just like in the training replica, we saw seven prisoners. The one in the middle was by far the oldest and weakest looking. We quickly descended a set of stairs which led to the dirt floor and approached the man in the middle who looked up at us helplessly. His arms and feet were both shackled in iron cuffs—the foot cuffs attached to a metal stake in the ground and the handcuffs mounted to the wall.

"Tommy?" I said softly.
"Who are you?" he answered weakly.
"It's Daniel McGunny."
"From back home?"
"Yes, and this is Mitchell, and we are here to rescue you and bring you back to Spring Falls."
"But how…"

Before he could finish his question, I commanded, "Free-eth. Free-eth. Free-eth. Free-eth." His shackles broke open. Tommy held his arms up and looked at his newly freed wrists.

"Free me!"

"Help me!"

"What about us?"

I heard the other prisoners yelling in our direction. I looked at Mitchell. "The king said just Tommy." I nodded in agreement.

"C'mon, Tommy, we have to move." We helped him to his feet, and the poor guy could barely stand. He was much taller than we were, so it was hard for us to help him. But he put his arms over our shoulders, and we did our best. We half-dragged him, and he half-walked up the steps. When we reached the top of the stairs, the two guards were still frozen. "Freezeth! Freezeth!" I hit them both again. This seemed almost too easy. We turned to the right to head back down the hallway when I heard a shrill laugh from behind us…

"Ha ha ha, it is true, what I have heard of your powers!" My head snapped around, and I was staring at the most beautiful—but scary—woman that I had ever seen. She was very tall. She had long wavy black hair and piercing green eyes. Her low-cut dress with fluffy shoulder pads was yellow on top and purple with gold vertical stripes on the lower gown. She also wore a bright-gold spiked crown with a giant red gem in the center, and she was holding a wand that looked a lot like mine. She pointed her wand at the ground and began levitating above the floor. She was hovering ten feet off the ground, maliciously looking down at us.

"The queen," Mitchell whispered in my direction, confirming my dreadful instincts.

"Mitchell Shrewsberry!" the queen said loudly, looking toward the sky. "King Salvatore's pet gnome!" Mitchell huffed, never taking his eyes off her, but he was able to bite his tongue. "Is your king really stupid enough to think that he is the only one with spies? We have been waiting for this day. What took you so long?"

I then heard a different woman's voice from behind me. "Kill them all and take his wand!" I turned and saw a younger woman, maybe eighteen to twenty years old. She had blond hair and blue eyes, she wore a much smaller crown and a cream-colored ankle-length dress with a brown rope belt. She held a bow and arrow and had a quiver with more arrows strapped to her back. Even more threatening was the evil look she gave us. In fact, there was an aura of evil all about her.

"Now, now, Princess Gabriella, let's not be too hasty." The queen looked us up and down. "Well, I definitely have no use for this one." She pointed her wand at Mitchell. She flicked her wrist and, with cold-blooded indifference said, "Killeth."

At that very moment, a brown flash hit the queen's shoulder, sending her flying across the floor. The arrow that left her wand whizzed over our heads and hit the stone wall behind us, ricocheting harmlessly to the ground. I looked back at the queen and saw King Salvatore on top of her. He had knocked the wand out of her hand, and it too slid across the floor.

"Go!" he yelled to us. Mitchell grabbed Tommy and me and began pulling us toward the corridor, which led to the short wall where we had planned to meet the king. Meanwhile, the princess started running toward the queen's wand.

"Wait!" I screamed and pointed Wanda at the running princess. "Freezeth!" I shouted, and the light traveled directly toward her. The princess cowered, preparing for impact. At that very moment, from under the king, Queen Kathelina held her hand out, and her wand shot across the floor right back into her outstretched fingers.

Almost simultaneously, she yelled, "Protecteth!" And a green shield flashed in front of the princess, absorbing my spell. The king pushed off the queen and flew straight up. We turned and started running again. The queen then turned toward her guards and shouted, "Free-eth! Free-eth!" Instantly, both guards were free and were running after us.

"Killeth! Killeth! Killeth!" The queen kept firing desperate shots at the flying, zigzagging king. I looked over my shoulder and saw the guards chasing us and preparing to launch their spears. Behind them was Princess Gabriella, looking for a shot with her bow.

Tommy was deadweight, and there was no way we would be able to outrun the guards and the princess. "Get Tommy to Sergeant Bernard!" I yelled to Mitchell, and then stopped and turned toward the trio that was chasing us. "Freezeth! Freezeth! Freezeth!" I hit all three of them. I hit both guards seconds before they were able to launch their spears, but the princess was able to fire her weapon before she was frozen. In all of the commotion, I didn't see where the arrow went, but when I turned around to run, I saw Mitchell facedown on the ground. Tommy was looking at me helplessly after he had seen what had happened. The arrow was sticking out of Mitchell's right shoulder.

"Mitchell!" I heard Prince Hugh scream. Mitchell rolled over onto his uninjured side. The arrow was sticking out the front of him right above the chest. "Are you okay?" the prince screamed in a panic.

"I...I think so," Mitchell was able to answer, gasping as he held his left hand over the wound with the arrow between his index and middle fingers. Blood was starting to drip from underneath his armor. Just then, Sergeant Bernard, Private Edwards, and another winged soldier swooped in and lifted the three of us over the wall. After landing, we immediately started toward the woods and General McGill's army. Sergeant Bernard and Hugh helped Mitchell, and the other two soldiers helped Tommy. I turned around and saw the aerial army protecting the castle exit. Spears and arrows flew toward the castle, and the queen's magic and arrows rocketed into the sky. Aerial soldiers were being struck, and one by one, they were falling lifelessly to the ground. When I looked back toward the tree line, I saw the ground army. By the time we approached General McGill, Tommy could hardly stand. Mitchell was seriously wounded, and the aerial army was beginning to weaken.

Chapter 27

We were about fifty feet away when—

"Soldiers, halt!" General McGill barked. One by one, starting from the left end, the soldiers stopped and spun their spears, holding them horizontally waist high. There were about fifty soldiers in the front row. I looked back toward the castle and saw the battle continuing.

We were now standing side by side—the two soldiers, Tommy, Prince Hugh, Sergeant Bernard, Mitchell, and me—all facing the general. "What is going on, Mike?" Sergeant Bernard asked.

"It's pretty simple, Sergeant," General McGill answered. "I have reached my limit serving under King Salvatore." Sergeant Bernard tilted his head, confused, trying to understand where this was headed. The general continued, "The best I can do under the king is General McGill. Now, doesn't "King Michael McGill" sound much better?"

"What in the world are you talking about?" the sergeant asked.

"Queen Kathelina is looking for a king, and she has chosen me! Together, we will rule all of Annabellia!"

He abruptly turned to his army and commanded, "Row 2! Fire!" The second row of soldiers launched their spears in our direction. I fumbled, trying to raise Wanda.

"Protecteth!" I yelled, and the green shield shot out. Spears disintegrated into the rotating force field.

"Keep it going, Daniel!" Sergeant Bernard put his arms out, and we slowly backed away from the army. I looked to my left and was relieved to see Prince Hugh, Sergeant Bernard, and Mitchell all safely behind the shield. I looked to my right and Tommy was standing next to me. Unfortunately, next to Tommy, I saw Private Edwards and the other soldier on the ground, lifeless with spears in their bodies. I gasped in horror, but I knew I needed to continue concentrating on the shield. We proceeded to edge backward, trying to get away from General McGill's army. But my arm was getting tired, and I could see the shield weakening.

"I'm losing it!" I screamed in terror. "What do I do?"

"Listen to me, Daniel," Sergeant Bernard commanded. He was shouting so that I could hear him over all the commotion. The shield was making a loud whirring noise that was slowing down as it became weaker. The spears and arrows from the attack continued to explode into the green force field. Bernard continued, "Just when the shield is about to break, I need you to hit the army with a zaruna spell!" I looked at Mitchell, who was still holding the arrow that was in his shoulder, and he gave me a nod of encouragement. The sergeant went on, "Count to three just before you withdraw the force field, and we will all hit the ground. As soon as the fire leaves your wand, we will break to the left and head for those trees!" We all looked to the left and saw a tree line with no soldiers guarding it. "Everybody understand?" The four of us acknowledged Sergeant Bernard. I was about to lose the spell.

"I can't hold it much longer!" I yelled, terrified.

"Do it, Daniel!" commanded Sergeant Bernard.

"One, two—" I saw a spear coming directly for us, and I paused until it hit. "Three! Zaruna!" We all dove to the ground; and I held my wand straight out, still pointing toward the front line. The fireball exploded into the front line of soldiers. I felt sick to my stomach. I had never killed anything in my life. However, I was only able to study the destruction for a second when I heard Sergeant Bernard.

"Move! Move! Move!" We all leaped up and sprinted toward the woods. "We need another shield, Daniel!" I turned around and saw arrows and spears raining down.

"Protecteth!" Another green force field circled in front of us. It was big, and it was strong. The remaining troops began swarming in our direction. They were moving much faster than we were because of Tommy and Mitchell's weakened states, not to mention me having to walk backward.

Suddenly, the soldiers began falling. I looked up, and the aerial army led by King Salvatore was attacking McGill's army from above. And the traitors had no defense. The enemy was forced to redirect its artillery from us to the King's aerial attack. I cut the force field, turned, and we all ran to the tree line. Tommy was being helped by the sergeant, and Hugh and I assisted Mitchell. We entered the forest to the west. I looked back, and McGill's army had retreated into the eastern woods from which they originally emerged as King Salvatore's army followed them in. We saw some movement near the castle, and Sergeant Bernard pulled us behind the trees and out of sight. We rushed through the woods for a short distance until the sergeant told us to stop.

"Sit down a minute," Sergeant Bernard directed. "How's everyone doing?" He asked. Tommy looked weak, and Mitchell was pale.

"I don't think I can go on." Mitchell sounded defeated.

"Hold on a second," the sergeant said as he was looking at the ground. He bent over and picked up a stick. He snapped it so that it was about six inches long, and he handed it to Mitchell. "Bite this," he said. Mitchell put the stick in his mouth longways so that it was sticking out of both sides. "You ready?" Sergeant Bernard asked. Mitchell nodded. Sergeant Bernard grabbed the arrow that was protruding from Mitchell's shoulder and snapped it so that it was almost flush with his armor. Mitchell let out a loud groan and slumped to the ground.

"Mitchell!" I screamed quietly, if that was possible.

"Give him a minute, Daniel. He'll be okay." The sergeant assured me. "Prince, Daniel, stay here with Tommy and Mitchell. I will be right back." The sergeant hurried away. Mitchell started to move by the time Sergeant Bernard returned after just a few minutes. "Okay, it doesn't look like anyone is coming our way yet. We will continue away from the other armies and make our way around the perimeter of Annabellia. This will add some time to our journey, but it is the safest way."

Mitchell was sitting up now. "You guys will have to go without me. Tommy needs your help to make that distance, and I will be nothing but a hindrance. I don't want to slow you down. I will be putting you all in danger."

"NO!" I was adamant. I looked at Sergeant Bernard.

"Very well, Mitchell, as you wish." I could not believe that the sergeant was going to let him die.

"Absolutely not!" I cried as tears rolled down my dirty face. I looked at Sergeant Bernard. "He is coming with us. We can get him to Martha's village. It is on the way. She can take care of him." I continued to cry as I was arguing.

"It's okay, Daniel." Mitchell seemed to be looking into my soul. He meant it.

Sergeant Bernard pulled a water flask from his belt and handed it to Mitchell. "Take this, Mitchell. You are a brave man. I will inform the king of your valor."

Mitchell reached for the water bottle when I heard from behind me, "We are not leaving without him!" I turned and saw Prince Hugh, who had a determined look on his face. He was standing tall and looked strong and confident. "Mitchell comes with us. We will take him to the village that Daniel spoke of."

The sergeant started to argue his case. "But Prince Hugh, it will be hard enough getting Tommy back in his weakened state. We cannot afford to have to help two—"

"I am the prince, and I am telling you all right now that Mitchell Shrewsberry will not be left behind. Nobody under my watch will be left behind…period!" His wings appeared to flap a couple of times involuntarily. He looked at me and nodded. I smiled back at the prince. He seemed to be growing up right before our eyes.

"Very well, Your Royal Highness." It was easy to see that Sergeant Bernard did not like this decision, but an order was an order. "Let's move." He held his hand out to Mitchell's uninjured arm and helped him to his feet. "The prince and I will help Tommy. Daniel, you help Mitchell. C'mon, this way." The sergeant led us north, away from the battle which was still audible off in the distance.

Chapter 28

It wasn't long before we could no longer hear the battle between the former allies. We continued moving steadily, but Mitchell and Tommy were both getting weaker and slower by the minute. "Who has the map?" asked Sergeant Bernard.

"I do," Mitchell answered softly. He stopped walking and reached inside his armor to pull it out. Exhaustion took over, and he fell to a seated position on the ground as if the map was too heavy. Without looking, he held the map up, and Sergeant Bernard took it from his hand.

Sergeant Bernard was reading the map when he looked, over the top of it, at Mitchell. "We need to get that armor off him. It is draining what little strength he has left." Prince Hugh and I took the comment as an order, and we carefully lifted the heavy coat off Mitchell's torso. The broken arrow was still in his upper right shoulder area, and his white undershirt was now damp and red. Fresh blood continued to ooze from around the wooden arrow and trickled down until it was absorbed in his shirt.

Mitchell looked down at his wound and touched his blood-soaked shirt with his left hand. "This is not good," he said, still studying his injury.

"Where are we going?" Tommy actually spoke. I looked over, and he was sitting against a tree. The prince and I both looked to Sergeant Bernard for an answer.

"The plan was to go to a cave in the north region of Annabellia. However, General McGill and his army probably know the location of the cave. We will head that way anyway. We should be able to see the cave from a distance, and we can then determine if it is safe before we approach it. If McGill's army has arrived there first, we must come up with an alternate plan."

"No!" I barked. Everyone looked at me, surprised and confused. I continued, "We need to get to Martha's village. Mitchell can't make it another night. Martha can help him."

The prince looked at me and nodded. He then turned to Sergeant Bernard. "Agreed." He stepped toward the sergeant and held out his hand for the map. Sergeant Bernard handed it to Prince Hugh, who then walked over to Mitchell. "Where is Martha's village?" he asked. Mitchell looked at the map and pointed east of King Salvatore's castle. After examining the map, Prince Hugh stated, "There is no way we can get that far today." Sergeant Bernard was looking over his shoulder and nodded in agreement.

"Then we will travel through the night. I'm not stopping until Mitchell is safe," I stated with conviction.

All eyes turned to Tommy who stood up. He actually looked like he was gaining strength.

"Whatever it takes…I just want to get home."

"Okay," Sergeant Bernard said, still looking at the map, "instead of traveling north, we will head due east from here. We should reach the northern rafts of Lake Montville by early morning. We will cross the lake at that point to stay away from your castle," he nodded at Prince Hugh. "Once we are across the lake, we will go southeast until we reach the village." Not another word was said as we helped Mitchell to his feet and started walking east. Prince Hugh continued to help Mitchell as we followed Tommy, who was now walking on his own right behind Sergeant Bernard.

Chapter 29

The trek was slow and difficult. Mitchell was getting weaker, and we were slogging through the woods without a trail. We were completely relying on Sergeant Bernard's directional instincts. He would constantly look toward the sky and make adjustments to our path. Mitchell needed breaks, and they were becoming more and more frequent. We had been a couple hours into our journey when Mitchell's legs gave out completely, and he would have crumpled to the ground if we hadn't been supporting him. "Mitchell!" I screamed and shook him. He was breathing. But his eyes were closed, and he was unresponsive.

Sergeant Bernard looked at Prince Hugh, and the prince knew exactly what he was thinking. "We are not leaving him," the prince said with conviction.

"I know," the sergeant answered. I was sure Sergeant Bernard thought this was a mistake, but he also knew that he wouldn't win an argument on the matter. He looked at us. "Tommy, you sit down. The prince, Daniel, and I will gather wood for a stretcher." The sergeant held his hands about two to three feet apart and instructed us, "Look for sturdy sticks about this long."

We had enough wood within five minutes. Sergeant Bernard then reached into his satchel and pulled out some rope. He started tying the makeshift stretcher together like he did it every day. It was quite amazing. The stretcher had two long sticks on the outside and several shorter, thinner branches connecting the two of them. Sergeant Bernard left about two feet on both sides of the wooden stretcher to use as handles.

Once the stretcher was finished, we placed it next to Mitchell and lifted him onto it. He let out a groan. Sergeant Bernard had some rope left and used it to begin securing Mitchell to the stretcher when we heard a snap. It sounded like someone stepped on a branch. Sergeant Bernard put a finger to his lips in a shushing gesture. We all sat silently, and then heard voices. The sergeant motioned for all of us to get on the ground. Quietly, we all lay down on our bellies. Through the trees, I saw two of General McGill's soldiers. They were walking straight toward us. I slowly and silently reached down and removed Wanda from its sleeve. I looked over at Sergeant Bernard who put his hand out, signaling me to sit tight. He crawled toward the soldiers and scanned the entire area. I thought he was trying to determine if there were more than just two. He looked back at me and mouthed the word *freezeth*.

The soldiers were getting closer and were sure to see us any second. Just then, Mitchell let out a painful sigh. With this, the soldiers stopped, drew their swords, and looked in our direction. They headed directly toward us. Once they came around a wide tree, they were face-to-face with me. The closer one raised his sword and lunged toward me.

"Freezeth, freezeth!" I hit them both. They stood mid-step, like statues with their swords still drawn. Sergeant Bernard jumped up and scoured the area.

"Okay, I think they're alone. You three, take Mitchell and start that way." He pointed to the east away from the soldiers. "I will catch up." He pulled a dagger from his belt. I knew what was about to happen, and I didn't want to see it. Prince Hugh and I each grabbed one of the stretcher's handles and, without a word, started dragging Mitchell away from the doomed soldiers as Tommy followed behind us.

As the prince and I continued to pull Mitchell through the woods, he groaned with every bump we dragged him over, and unfortunately, there were a lot of them. I felt terrible that Mitchell was in pain, but every groan meant that he was still alive. After a short time, we heard footsteps behind us. We froze, then turned to see Sergeant Bernard appear from behind a tree. He nodded at us and asked, "Are you guys okay?"

The front of his uniform was covered in blood. I was staring at him with my mouth opened. He looked down at himself, then quickly assured us that it wasn't his. Nothing else about that matter needed to be discussed.

Sergeant Bernard walked over to us and put his hand across Mitchell's forehead. "He's cold." The sergeant looked around. "It is starting to get dark, and he will get colder. We need to keep him as warm as we can." Sergeant Bernard removed his bloody outer garment from his torso and laid it over Mitchell. "Here you go, my friend." He then said, "Drink," as he held his water flask to Mitchell's lips. Most of the water dribbled down the corners of Mitchell's mouth. But you could see him swallow, so we knew that he was able to consume a little.

"We have been going due east for some time, so we must start heading south now," the sergeant informed us. "We should reach Lake Montville by morning. I got this," he said as he grabbed the handles of the stretcher from Hugh and me. He then took a hard right turn and started heading south through the woods. Silently, we fell in line behind him and followed.

Chapter 30

We traveled quietly and uneventfully for the next few hours. Occasionally, we would come across a small stream and fill our water bottles. From time to time, we would stumble upon some braslowberry trees whose fruit provided us with food. The sergeant pulled the stretcher the entire time, refusing our offers to take a turn. "Just help Tommy" was his response every time. Mitchell was still moaning from time to time, but these moans were becoming less frequent. As night crept in, the sergeant asked if I had any spells for light.

"Try 'illuminateth, ill-lum-in-ate-eth,'" Prince Hugh suggested to me.

I pulled Wanda from its sleeve and held it out in front of me. "Okay, illuminateth." I flicked my wrist, but nothing happened. "Illuminateth!" Nothing.

Prince Hugh then said, "Try holding the wand straight out, but don't flick your wrist. Just hold the wand still."

I did exactly as he said, and a glowing sphere appeared at Wanda's white tip. The glowing ball was a soft whitish-yellow light, and it was about the size of a baseball. The sphere was far from bright, but it emitted enough light for us to see easily. Actually, it was perfect because it didn't seem like anyone would be able to see it from far away.

The night was slow and quiet. It was obvious that Tommy's fatigue had returned. He was trying to keep up, but his bare feet and malnourished old man's body were not a good combination. We were taking breaks more frequently, and after what seemed like days, it started to get brighter. I put Wanda back in its sleeve, and we kept moving.

Dawn was still creeping in when I heard what sounded like waves crashing on a shore. "Is that Lake Montville?" I asked excitedly.

"Yes, Daniel," the sergeant answered. I saw that we were close to the tree line, and through the breaks, I could see the blue water. "We need to stay in the woods for cover. If my estimates are correct, the raft ropes will be another hour or so south." He set Mitchell's stretcher on the ground. "Sit and rest, Tommy. Prince Hugh, Daniel, come with me." Tommy sat next to Mitchell and tried to give him some water. The prince and I walked over to Sergeant Bernard. He crept slowly to the tree line and looked out from behind a tree. "There they are! Much closer than I thought."

Prince Hugh and I peeked around the tree. Off in the distance, not more than a half mile away, were a line of rafts floating on the shore. The exhaustion that I was feeling instantly disappeared, and it was replaced with an energy I didn't think I had left. I was ready to go. "Once we cross, how long will it take us to get to the village?" I asked.

Sergeant Bernard answered, "An hour, maybe two. We should be there by the afternoon." Prince Hugh and I hugged each other with excitement. We all returned to Tommy and Mitchell. "How is he doing?" the sergeant asked Tommy.

"He's weak. He won't drink," Tommy answered sadly.

"Okay then, let's keep moving," the sergeant commanded. He grabbed the handles of the stretcher and started south just inside the tree line. We hiked for about fifteen minutes when Sergeant Bernard came to a halt. He put his hand up, telling us to stop and be quiet. Once still, we were able to hear voices off in the distance. The sergeant peeked out from the trees and looked around. I couldn't see much from where I was standing, but I could tell that there was about two hundred yards of grass between the forest and the lake. And we were probably about fifty feet uphill from the water.

Sergeant Bernard turned around and spoke to us, "Okay, the voices you hear are only those of the villagers. Tommy, how are you feeling?" Tommy gave the sergeant a thumbs-up with a nod. "Good. On my go, you and the prince will take Mitchell down the hill to the rafts. Daniel, you will follow them backward. Have your wand ready just in case Queen Kathelina or McGill's army are waiting for us. Face the forest and watch for any enemies that may appear." I nodded. "Good. I will look out and defend from the sky. Are we ready?" We all shook our heads yes.

We approached the last trees between us and the lake, and I looked out. Down the hill, there was a line of five rafts attached to a rope—just like the one Mitchell and I used to cross Lake Montville the first time.

"Get out to that first raft and start crossing the lake. I will fly out and meet you when I think you are clear. Ready? Go!" Sergeant Bernard took a step and flew out of the woods, and then shot straight into the air. Tommy and Prince Hugh, each holding a stretcher handle, started a slow run down the hill, dragging Mitchell toward the rafts. I backed out of the woods, never taking my eyes off the tree line. I looked back and forth, north and south as I backed down the hill. Sergeant Bernard was floating about fifty feet up in the sky, watching the same tree line as I was. After a minute or two, I looked over my shoulder and saw that the other three had reached the rafts.

Before I could even look back, I heard Sergeant Bernard scream, "Daniel!" I immediately turned and saw a wave of soldiers rushing out of the forest. "Go!" the sergeant yelled as he started firing arrow after arrow down at the army from the sky. I turned and sprinted to the rafts. The others had already reached the far raft, and Prince Hugh and Tommy were yelling at me to hurry. I stepped on the first raft and almost fell as it wobbled in the water. I bear-crawled across the other rafts until I reached the far one which was holding my friends. As I turned around, the army was approaching the shoreline.

"Fire!" I heard, and without even thinking, I spun around and put up a protecteth spell.

"Pull!" I heard Prince Hugh yell as he and Tommy started pulling the rope and propelling the raft. Meanwhile, the soldiers were scrambling to get to the raft behind us. I looked through my green shield and saw that General McGill was leading the charge. We had probably traveled about a hundred feet from shore when the second raft with General McGill started skimming toward us.

They had the strength of five or six soldiers pulling on their rope, while we had Prince Hugh and a nine-year-old

old man pulling ours. I wasn't able to help the two of them because the arrows were raining down on us and I needed to maintain the shield. Clearly, it wouldn't be long before we were overtaken by McGill and his soldiers. On the shore, additional soldiers were piling into the other three rafts and launching toward us.

With a swoosh and a thud, Sergeant Bernard landed on our raft and urgently joined in pulling the rope. General McGill was still gaining on us but not as fast. Still, there was no way we were going to make it all the way across the lake without being overwhelmed by the soldiers. "Should I zaruna their butts?" I yelled to Sergeant Bernard.

"You cannot break your shield as long as they are firing at us. If there is a break, then go for it!" he yelled back. We were not even halfway across the big lake, and General McGill was now within twenty feet of us.

"All we want is the wand, Daniel! Give us the wand, and we will let you go!" General McGill yelled from his raft. I knew I couldn't give it to him because without Wanda, not only would I lose my magic, rendering us helpless, but Tommy and I could never go home.

Just then, the water started bubbling and a giant reptilian head blasted from under the surface. Junkita looked at us. Her eyes were drawn down to Mitchell. Then she looked at the rafts behind us. She gave an angry snort, belching two puffs of smoke from her nostrils. Then, barely making a splash, she disappeared back under the water.

Sergeant Bernard, Tommy and Prince Hugh, regardless of what they just witnessed, never stopped pulling us across the lake. They were expending every ounce of energy that they had. Suddenly, about twenty feet behind us, Junkita exploded out of the water. She flapped her giant green wings as she stared down at General McGill and his men. Throwing her head back, she let out a violent roar that sent vibrations through our bodies. Accompanying the roar was a blast of fire shooting straight into the air with a force we could feel twenty feet away. She then dropped her head and fired the powerful flames at General McGill's raft. The soldiers screamed in terror and pain as they were burned alive. Some attempted to save themselves by diving into the water.

A charred General McGill collapsed and dropped to his knees on the raft. Junkita then lowered her head, bared her teeth, and ensnared General McGill in her giant mouth. She threw her head back like a human swallowing an aspirin, and just like that, McGill was gone.

The flames had burned through the rope, and McGill's raft was now floating empty without direction. The surviving soldiers on the other three rafts were trying to pull themselves back to the opposite shore, but they never made it. Junkita lit them up, sending all of them to their burning watery graves.

Junkita settled back into the water and swam toward us. She submerged herself at the rear of the raft, and then resurfaced so that the raft was sitting on her back. Balancing the raft, she swam us all the way across Lake Montville until we were about a hundred feet from shore. Sergeant Bernard was then able to reach a floating rope that was still attached to a tree on the shoreline.

Before Sergeant Bernard began pulling us to shore, Junkita brought her giant head down to my eye level. She looked at all of us, paused, and then soaked me with that big old wet tongue of hers. I heard a quiet chuckle from Mitchell who had his eyes closed but a smirk on his face.

After Junkita disappeared below the surface of the lake, Sergeant Bernard pulled us ashore. We climbed off the raft and entered the woods. As soon as we were out of sight, we all collapsed from physical and mental exhaustion.

Chapter 31

We rested in silence for about five minutes, trying to digest the carnage that we had just witnessed. Finally, Sergeant Bernard spoke, "I think we are safe here. Let's make a fire. We need to eat."

"No!" I protested. "We need to get Mitchell to Martha's village right away."

"I agree with Daniel," Prince Hugh concurred. Sergeant Bernard looked at me, looked at Mitchell, and grudgingly pulled out the map.

"It looks like we are about an hour north of the village." He then looked at Tommy: "Can you make it?" Tommy nodded. "All right then, let's get moving." We all stood up slowly like we were eighty years old—well, I guess Tommy kind of was. Sergeant Bernard grabbed the stretcher and started through the woods. Tommy, the prince, and I followed in single file behind him. It wasn't long before we came across a trail.

"Don't move," the sergeant ordered, and we all stopped. He took off from the ground and flew straight up between the trees. We could barely see him through the branches, but it looked like he was turning slowly. After only a minute or so, he floated back down. "It looks safe. I didn't see anything or anyone following us." With a little feeling of relief, we continued onward to Martha's village.

It wasn't long before we reached the edge of the forest and stepped out of the woods into the hidden town where Martha had welcomed us not so long ago. However, there was a very different feeling to the village this time. I did not see a soul in the streets. All the tiny houses were buttoned up, and all the colorful shutters and doors were shut tightly. I pointed to Martha's house, and we headed toward it.

Suddenly, Martha's green door flew open, and she came running toward us. "Mitchell!" she screamed. "Is he all right?" We all looked at her. We didn't know how to answer. I looked down at Mitchell, and he was unresponsive. I looked back at Martha, speechless, with an empty stare on my face.

Martha looked around at the other houses and shouted, "Doctor McGee! Doctor McGee!" A door to the house on our right slowly opened, and a gentleman peeked out. Martha pleaded, "It's Mitchell! He's hurt!"

An older man wearing mostly black stepped out, looking in all directions. He used a cane, not a magic one like mine but a walking stick like Mitchell's. He approached us and laid his hand on Mitchell's forehead. "Take him inside, Martha," he ordered. "I will get my bag."

While the doctor returned to his house, Martha led us into her cottage, and we took Mitchell off his stretcher and placed him in the same bed that he had just slept in a few nights ago. Martha pulled up a chair next to his bed and grabbed his hand. She laid her head down on the bed next to their intertwined hands. The sergeant, prince, and

Tommy retreated to the kitchen. Silently, I stood next to Martha until the doctor entered with his bag. "Please let me have the room," he said sympathetically to Martha. She stood, slowly letting go of Mitchell's hand, and we exited the room together.

When we entered the kitchen, the other three stood up. "Would you like some tea or something to eat?" Martha asked.

The sergeant responded, "Thank you, ma'am. But we have put you in enough danger, so we should leave. We need to get Tommy to the gateway before the queen and her army find us."

"Yes, we have heard of the great battles, but you must rest a minute and eat something. We will keep our village locked up, and they will never know that you were here."

Sergeant Bernard looked at Prince Hugh. The prince nodded, saying, "Tommy needs to eat."

"Thank you, ma'am," the sergeant said looking at Martha. "We would be grateful for a quick bite, and then we will be on our way." Martha instantly went to work, and we had full meals sitting in front of us within minutes. Tommy ate like he hadn't seen food in years. Sadly, he probably hadn't. Quickly, we finished our delicious meals and drank our braslowberry tea. Sergeant Bernard then stood up and said, "Thank you for your hospitality, ma'am. We must be on our way." The rest of us stood up and, one by one, thanked Martha. As the others started toward the door, I walked over to the bedroom. The others stopped and watched me while I peeked in at Mitchell and the doctor. I stood in the doorway, made the sign of the cross, and turned and walked back to my companions.

"Daniel," Martha said as we were exiting the house. I turned and looked at her. "Mitchell would never have put you in danger if he had known what would happen."

"I know," I said. "Please take care of him." Martha ran across the room and gave me a giant hug. Emotions overtook me, and I began sobbing. It was like Martha's embrace opened up a floodgate of feelings that I had been suppressing ever since Mitchell took a turn for the worse.

"I'll worry about Mitchell," she said, still squeezing me. "You get Tommy and yourself safely home."

"I will," I answered, not fully believing myself. The hug ended, and I turned and walked out the door with my head down and my shoulders slumped. Martha watched us exit, and then closed the door behind us.

Chapter 32

We had just entered the forest when we heard a clamor from the other side of the village. We quickly took cover and looked back. "Holy crap," I whispered. We were staring directly at Queen Kathelina herself, who was flanked by Princess Gabriella and about ten soldiers.

"Inhabitants of this village, I command you to open your doors!" the queen belted out in a voice loud enough for all to hear. Shutters began opening, and the apprehensive villagers peeked out.

Princess Gabriella walked down the center of the village shouting, "The queen ordered you to open your doors, not your windows. Anyone who does not obey shall be punished." One by one, the doors began to open. People stood in each doorway. A couple of children nervously clung to their parents' legs. I looked at Martha's cottage, and she too was standing in her doorway.

The queen spoke, "We are looking for two humans and a man like you who goes by the name of Mitchell. Has anyone seen them?" The queen, princess, and soldiers' eyes scoured the people in their doorways. There was no response from anyone. She continued, "There will be a reward for anyone who helps us, and there will be punishment for anyone who harbors or aids the fugitives." Again, they looked around and heard no response from the villagers. The queen continued, "Very well. We will search every house in the village. If we find anything in any single house…the entire village will be burned to the ground." The queen walked into the first house that she came upon. The princess entered a house with children in the doorway; and soldiers in pairs entered several other houses, including Martha's.

"We must go," Sergeant Bernard whispered.

"Right," the prince agreed. Slowly and quietly, we crept deeper into the forest. Once we felt we were at a safe distance, we started to move as fast as Tommy could run. He actually moved at a decent pace considering everything that he had been through. Maybe it was the food, maybe it was the thought of getting home, or maybe it was because the queen was right on our tails. Regardless, I was just happy that we were making decent time. Happy for us; but terrified for Mitchell, Martha, and the rest of the villagers.

"What are they gonna do?" I asked out loud to no one in particular.

"If they are anything like Mitchell, then there is no doubt that they are a savvy group of villagers, Daniel," Sergeant Bernard answered. "Have faith. I'm sure they will think of something." I wasn't sure if he believed that or if he was just appeasing me, but I knew that there was nothing that we could do at this point except keep moving forward.

We raced through the woods until we arrived at the clearing leading to the mountains of Magnolia and their ominous cliffs. We stopped and looked up. It was a much different sight this time. Only one loloster was perched on a ledge near the top of the highest peak. "I'm not even sure that he can see us," I said, like I was an expert.

"Okay," the prince answered, "let's get to that first hut." The prince stepped out onto the grass field, and Tommy was nudged by Sergeant Bernard to follow. The sergeant then nodded at me to go, and he stepped out right behind me. Before we knew it, the four of us were safely in the first hut. We looked up through the skylight and saw that the loloster hadn't budged. Encouraged by this, we quickly made our way to the second, third, and fourth huts without incident. Suddenly, the loloster purposely swooped off the ledge and began gliding downward. It then circled the field at a much lower level than the ledge upon which he had been perched.

"As soon as he circles away from us, we need to go," Sergeant Bernard commanded. We all looked at one another and nodded. "Now!" he shouted, and we burst out of the hut in the same order and dashed to the fifth hut.

"Stop right there!" we heard someone yell from the field behind us. When we looked over our shoulders, we could see the queen, the princess, and their soldiers grouped at the edge of the forest. The loloster had also heard the queen's command and reacted by diving toward the sound.

This was just the distraction we needed. "Go!" yelled Prince Hugh. He and Tommy led the way to the sixth and final hut. After reaching it, I looked out the back door and saw the queen and her entourage just arrive at the first hut.

I removed Wanda from its sleeve and commanded, "Zaru! Zaru! Zaru!" firing three flaming balls back in the direction of the queen. Each one exploded, one hitting the second hut and the other two blasting the rock mountains on both sides.

"Go!" I heard the prince yell again, and we were off and headed toward the entrance of Dee Dee's Dark Wood Forest. Once in the forest, I looked up and saw a mass of lolosters darkening the sky. They began dive bombing the hut occupied by the queen and company, so temporarily, the enemy was trapped. But the queen was soon at the doorway with her wand firing into the sky. One by one, lolosters dropped from the air.

"We must move," said Sergeant Bernard. "That won't slow them down for long." We turned and raced through the woods, following the trail which led to the Bridge of Dee Dee. It was no longer the "Skinny" Bridge of Dee Dee. My earlier "reconstruction" had remade it into the Grand Bridge of Dee Dee. We scurried across the new bridge, and when we reached the other side, the prince stopped.

"You two keep moving," he said to Tommy and the sergeant. "Daniel and I will be right behind you." He then turned to me and instructed, "Hold your wand out, make a small circle, flick your wrist, and say 'destructeth maximas.'" I looked at him puzzled. "Do it, Daniel!" he ordered. I held my arm straight out, pointed at the bridge, made a circle, flicked my wrist, and—"Destructeth maximas!" A silver ball shot from my wand and headed toward the middle of the bridge. The ball kept growing as it neared its target and *boom*! The ball exploded into the center of the bridge. The bridge blew apart in the middle; and the entire structure crumbled and fell, crashing into the river below. So much for the Grand Bridge of Dee Dee. Just then the queen, princess, and soldiers appeared from the dark woods across the canyon.

"Killeth!" I heard her yell, and an arrow came streaming in our direction.

"Protecteth!" I commanded Wanda, and a spinning green shield appeared from its tip. *Pfft*, the shield gobbled up the arrow. We walked backward for a minute, and when it was clear that the queen wasn't going to fire again, we turned and ran. We caught up to Sergeant Bernard and Tommy in no time.

"Good thinking, Prince!" the sergeant said with a smile. "That should buy us some time." The sergeant was right—it was a good call. The prince had really impressed me throughout the day. He was not afraid to give orders or implement strategies. He was wise beyond his years. There was no doubt in my mind that he was indeed going to make a good king someday. Prince Hugh grinned proudly, and we kept moving.

Chapter 33

Soon, we were making our way through open pastures when I saw that beautiful waterfall in the distance. As we approached the waterfall, we heard a loud noise far behind us. It sounded familiar. Then I realized it was similar to the sound Wanda made when I created the new bridge during our journey to the king's castle.

Sergeant Bernard confirmed my suspicions. "She just rebuilt the bridge." I looked at Tommy as he trudged ahead, and he now seemed tired. He was leaning on his walking stick with every step, and he grimaced every time he pushed off on it. "How are you doing?" the sergeant asked him.

"I'm okay. I'll be fine," Tommy answered.

We all knew that the queen and her company were much faster than we were, and we didn't feel the need to remind ourselves of it. We pressed onward and passed the waterfall. The sun was starting to set, and I was hoping that we could get to the gateway by Mitchell's house before dark. As slow as Tommy was, we were definitely moving faster than Mitchell and I did on our way out.

"Keep moving," Sergeant Bernard ordered as he sailed straight up into the air. He wasn't up there long when he floated back down and informed us, "They're gaining on us." We all felt the urgency, but Tommy was really struggling. We needed to move even faster than we had been, but Tommy was running on empty now.

We pushed forward, but when it became too much for Tommy, he crumpled to the ground in a heap with his face down. "Tommy!" the prince yelled as we rolled him over. Tommy's eyes rolled back in his head, and he didn't answer. His eyes just fluttered.

Sergeant Bernard shot up toward the sky but hadn't risen twenty feet when he came right back down. "They're coming." He looked at me. "How much farther, Daniel?"

I was trying to think. I thought we were close but admitted, "I'm not exactly sure."

The prince chimed in. "Less than a mile due east," he stated confidently. "The gateway is in a tree trunk adjacent to Mitchell's house."

"Very well. Put Tommy on my back," he ordered as he knelt down next to him.

"You can't carry him that far," the prince said.

"We don't have a choice," barked Sergeant Bernard.

"All right, Daniel, give me a hand." We were able to get Tommy on the sergeant's back. "You need to hold on," Prince Hugh said to Tommy as he gave him a soft slap across the face to rouse him. Tommy let out a small groan and clasped his hands around Sergeant Bernard's neck.

"Here we go!" The sergeant ran for about twenty steps and leaped into the air. He struggled to gain any height but finally was able to get about ten feet off the ground. His wings flapped as the two of them wobbled like a small plane trying to take off in a windstorm.

The queen, princess, and soldiers were now visible and gaining on us. They must have seen us too because they picked up their pace and began running straight toward us. I removed Wanda from its sleeve as Prince Hugh and I darted in the direction of the gateway. Soon, I was able to make out Mitchell's house growing larger as we got closer. Just then, Sergeant Bernard and Tommy crashed to the ground, rolling and sliding to a stop on their backs. I wasn't 100 percent sure, but it looked like they were only a few yards away from the gateway. Sergeant Bernard was able get to his knees and was trying to help Tommy up.

The prince and I sprinted to Tommy and Sergeant Bernard as the enemy closed in on us. As we raced to the finish line, the prince reminded me. "Remember that Tommy's hand must be on the wand to get through the gateway."

"Got it!" I replied. When we reached Tommy, we were less than twenty feet from the gateway. We barely broke stride as both the prince and I each grabbed one of Tommy's arms and started dragging him as his feet clumsily tried to keep up. Sergeant Bernard was still on his knees, exhausted and unable to help anymore. He collapsed on the ground as we dragged Tommy away. We were in reach of the gateway, and I had Wanda out in front of me.

"Killeth!" I heard Queen Kathelina shriek.

"Daniel, look out!" I heard a deep voice yell from above. I swung my wand around and saw a brown blur flash in front of us, moving from left to right.

"Protecteth!" I created a green shield in front of Tommy, the prince, and me. Looking down, I could see I wasn't hit. I glanced at Tommy and Prince Hugh; and they were still standing, uninjured. I then looked at the ground to my right and saw King Salvatore lying on the ground. An arrow was protruding from the left side of his chest. I hadn't raised my shield in time, and he had taken the hit himself to protect us. He was on his back, struggling to breath, but he was able to turn and look at us as he held his arm out in our direction. I kept the shield up.

"I am sorry, Daniel," the king said panting. "Please… protect…my son." He then looked at Hugh and said, "You…will be…a great king…I will…always…be…watching." His arm fell to the ground. His eyes closed, and his breathing ceased.

"NOOOOO!" Hugh screamed.

"We gotta move," I screeched at Prince Hugh, trying to distract him from his father's lifeless body. I started to back up to the tree, which housed the gateway, but I couldn't lower my shield yet.

"I will have that wand!" Queen Kathelina demanded over the whirring buzz of my shield. She had reached Sergeant Bernard. The queen bent over, grabbed him, and yanked him to his feet. She had her wand pointed at the side of his head as she held him in a choke hold with her other arm. Princess Gabriella flanked her right side.

An evil smile of victory stretched across the princess's face. "Give us the wand, and you can all go free." She started to approach us.

"We can't do it, Daniel," Prince Hugh said to me.

"Don't do it, Daniel!" Sergeant Bernard quietly growled.

I looked around. "Okay, okay," I said, addressing the queen, "you can have it."

"What are you doing, Daniel?" the prince snarled.

"No, Daniel. Don't!" the sergeant pleaded.

Princess Gabriella laughed triumphantly as she whipped her head back and looked to the sky like an evil villain from a cartoon.

While she celebrated, I whispered to Tommy, "When I say 'now,' grab the wand, and whatever happens, do not let go." I then shouted to Queen Kathelina, "Bring the sergeant to me, and I will let you have the wand."

"Daniel, what are you doing?" the prince questioned again.

"If we go through the gateway, she will kill all of you," I responded. "Trust me."

The queen slowly approached. She was still holding Sergeant Bernard with the wand still pointed at his head. "Lower your shield, Daniel, and drop the wand."

"Let go of Sergeant Bernard and put your wand away," I demanded.

Queen Kathelina continued her tentative approach, still not releasing Sergeant Bernard. "Lower your shield," she again demanded.

"Let him go," I repeated.

The queen slowly lowered her wand and shoved Sergeant Bernard in our direction. I flicked my wrist, and the shield disappeared. In the same instant, I moved toward the tree trunk and plunged the wand into the gateway hole. Tommy now stood on one side of the protruding wand while I was on the other. Prince Hugh was next to Tommy. I then let go of the wand and held my hands in the air. "It's yours," I said to the queen.

As the queen approached the trunk, ready to reach for the wand, she looked at Tommy and said, "You had such promise, Tommy. I would have kept you young and strong, but you chose to betray me. As for you, Daniel, I could use a young man with your powers. Think about it." She greedily grabbed onto the wand.

"Now!" I yelled at Tommy. Before the queen could react, Tommy grabbed onto the wand. Simultaneously, I reached out, gripped Wanda, and twisted it.

Bam! Instantly, the three of us were standing in the creek back home in Spring Falls, Ohio. I looked at Tommy and saw that he had transformed back into a nine-year-old. The queen, on the other hand, screamed as she began aging decades by the second. She was actually disintegrating right before our eyes. With her final fading scream and a muffled *poof*, her golden crown fell to the ground. The only thing left of her was a cloud of black dust that drifted away and dissipated in the October breeze.

Meanwhile, deep in the castle of Lordstown, Queen Margaret's eyes fluttered and opened for the first time in years.

SEAN O'NEILL

Chapter 34

"Holy crap!" Tommy yelled. He looked down at himself, examining his rejuvenated body. He couldn't have been happier. He was nine years old again.

I didn't give him much time to celebrate. I bent down and picked up the crown. "We have to go back, Tommy," I said with concern in my voice.

"What! No way!"

"Tommy, just for a minute."

"Why?" He sounded distraught, no, terrified.

"We need to show everyone that we are both alive and safe and let them know that the queen is dead. The crown will be the proof. He didn't seem convinced, so I reassured him. "We're in no danger anymore. You saw the queen disintegrate. Nothing can hurt us there now, and we'll only stay a few minutes. Now grab on…please."

Reluctantly, Tommy shuffled over, looked at Wanda, and then at me. "Just for a minute?" he asked.

"Just for a minute. I promise." We both grabbed the wand.

Poof! We were back in Annabellia. Princess Gabriella and the soldiers were still there, but by this time, Sergeant Bernard had been reinforced by the aerial army who were surrounding the princess and her soldiers. I also noticed that Tommy had become old again.

I then saw Prince Hugh, kneeling next to the king's body, which had been covered with a blanket. Tommy and I walked over and stood on either side of the prince. We both placed a hand on his shoulders and knelt down next to him. The prince looked at me. His eyes were swollen from crying, and his cheeks were crusty with a mixture of dirt and tears. A tear rolled down my right cheek as I paid my respects with a silent stare.

"Where is the queen?" I heard the shrill voice of Princess Gabriella yell.

I stood up and turned to face everyone. I walked to where I could see them all and proclaimed, "Queen Kathelina is dead!" I held her crown high above my head to show the proof.

"It was awesome!" Tommy belted out. "She got a thousand years old in seconds and turned into dust right in front of our eyes!"

Shocked, Princess Gabriella gasped and sat on the ground while the aerial army erupted into cheers. The prince stood up and solemnly approached me. He wrapped his arms around me and squeezed me so hard that I could hardly breathe. "Thank you, Daniel," he whispered in my ear. He let go of me and looked at Tommy. "Are you all right?" Tommy nodded at the prince.

Sergeant Bernard approached Prince Hugh. "What are your orders, sir?"

The prince pointed at Princess Gabriella. "Return to your castle, free all your prisoners, and stay there. If you or any of your soldiers venture outside of your castle walls, there will be consequences." He then looked at Sergeant Bernard. "All of General McGill's soldiers are guilty of treason. Any of them found will be arrested and punished."

"Yes, sir," Sergeant Bernard bowed at the prince.

Prince Hugh looked back at Princess Gabriella. "Go! Before I change my mind." The princess and her soldiers turned and dejectedly retreated across the field until they disappeared into the forest.

Sergeant Bernard approached me. He reached into his pocket and pulled out a small vile and handed it to me. "Mitchell told me to make sure Tommy drinks this when you get back through your gateway. It's supposed to help him heal or something. I don't know." I took it from his hand, and then thanked him for all he had done for us.

Then I looked at the prince. "I need to get Tommy home." Prince Hugh nodded in agreement. "I will return as soon as possible. I need to check on Mitchell."

The prince replied, "You worry about Tommy. I will send someone to the village immediately to check on Mitchell."

"Daniel, can we please go now?" Tommy was getting antsy.

"Of course, Tommy. Let's go." I nodded at Prince Hugh and Sergeant Bernard. I placed the wand in the hole. "Grab on," I instructed Tommy, and just like that, we were back in the creek. I handed Tommy the vile. "Sergeant Bernard got this from Mitchell. I guess it's supposed to help you heal or something."

Without questioning, he opened it, shrugged his shoulders, and drank it. "I can't believe I'm home," Tommy said, smiling from ear to ear. He burped, grabbed his stomach, and complained, "I'm not feeling so well." He sat down on a big rock. His eyes rolled back in his head, and then he fell backward.

"Tommy!" I ran over and began shaking him. Within seconds, Tommy blinked a few times and opened his eyes.

"What the hell are you doing?" Tommy sat up and pushed me away. "Get your hands off me, McGunny!"

I looked at him confused. "Are you okay? Do you want me to walk you home?" I asked.

"I know where I live, you freak. Now leave me alone!"

"Tommy, are you all right?" I asked.

"Jesus, McGunny, will you just get away from me?"

"Don't you remember anything, Tommy?"

"I remember you're a giant tool!" Tommy stood up and brushed himself off. He climbed up the creek bed and walked toward the baseball game that I had been a part of before this crazy adventure.

"Hey, it's the Anderson kid!" I heard someone yell. Everyone who was playing immediately erupted, screaming with excitement. I watched from the bushes, trying to avoid being seen. The baseball game ended immediately, and my brother and all his friends followed a confused Tommy home. I left in the opposite direction and took the long way back to my house. After all I had been through, I still made it home in plenty of time for my birthday dinner.

Chapter 35

I went back to the creek the next morning about fifteen hours after I had returned home. I did the math and figured I had been gone for two and a half years in Annabellia time. I wondered what I would now find. I stuck my wand in the gateway hole, and back in Annabellia I was. I got my bearings and saw Mitchell's house. I sprinted to his door. I knocked and called out for Mitchell, but there was no response. I put my wand in the door latch and took a deep breath. I twisted Wanda, and Mitchell's door flung open. There was no one inside. I looked around, and there were cobwebs everywhere. The house was incredibly dusty, but other than that, it was exactly as we had left it when we had headed out on our journey. My heart sank. Sadly, I closed the door behind me and started for the castle.

I had eaten a big breakfast back home, so I didn't intend to stop until I reached Martha's house. I traveled across familiar pastures and past the waterfall. I made it through Dee Dee's Dark Wood Forest, and I blew past the lolosters with no problems. Soon, I arrived at Martha's village. I walked out the woods into the little social courtyard and heard someone say, "You are Mitchell's friend."

I looked over and recognized Franklin, the man whom I had met the first time we arrived at the village. "Yes, I'm Daniel. Is Mitchell…I mean have you seen…"

"Don't worry, Daniel. Mitchell is alive and well. He is at the king's castle. He is the king's right-hand man now."

"How was he able to avoid the queen and her soldiers?" I asked.

"Two soldiers entered Martha's house right after you left. Doctor McGee was still there. Doc told the guards that the man in bed was Martha's husband who was very sick and very contagious. Ha ha, the guards never made it past the bedroom door."

"Outstanding," I replied. "Is Martha home?'

"No, son, Martha does not live in our village anymore either." I looked at Franklin confused and concerned.

"It is traditional for a woman to live with her husband, especially if her husband works for the king." He smiled and winked at me.

I was overjoyed. "Thank you, sir, I am off to the castle."

"Nice to see you again, Daniel."

"Nice to see you too." We shook hands, and I exited the village.

I was so elated I almost skipped down the trail to the lake. I pulled a raft across Lake Montville. Well, I may have had a little help from Wanda. As I crossed, I was a little disappointed as well as a little relieved that I didn't see Junkita. Once I reached the other side of the lake, I jumped off the raft and continued on my way until I arrived at Lordstown. I approached the gate and was greeted by two guards.

I made my way to the center of the stone city. As I neared the castle, I was approached by two sentinels. They were wearing armor and carrying swords. One of them spoke, "Daniel McGunny?"

They almost seemed to be expecting me. "Yes," I answered, confused.

"Please come with us." They led me to the castle, and then down a hallway to a sitting room. "Please have a seat." They showed me to a couch, and then disappeared around a corner. I sat there for a few minutes in silence, watching people pass by the doorway. Suddenly, loud bells began tolling, and several people began rushing around. I started to get a little nervous. But as quickly as the commotion in the castle had started, the hustle and bustle stopped, and the guards returned. "Please follow us," one stated. I stood up and walked behind them.

They led me down a long corridor to two grand doors. They each grabbed a door and simultaneously pulled them open to reveal a grand hall. It looked like a giant church. All the benches in the room were full of people, and every one of them was looking at me. At the end of a long red-carpeted aisle, standing on an altar-like structure was Prince Hugh. He still looked young, just like he did when I went home…yesterday. Next to him stood a beautiful woman. She was tall, dark-skinned, and had no hair. She was wearing elaborate makeup and had a gold crown on her head. She and the prince were both staring at me with big smiles across their faces.

"Daniel," I heard from behind. I turned around and saw Sergeant Bernard.

"Sergeant Bernard!" I exclaimed as I ran into his arms and hugged him as he knelt down to greet me.

"Actually, it's General Bernard now," he corrected me as he straightened his arms and let me go. "A lot has changed since we last saw you."

"Congratulations, General." I said, "I heard Mitchell and Martha got married."

"Indeed, they did," General Bernard said smiling.

"Who is that with Prince Hugh?"

"You mean King Hugh?" General Bernard said, stressing the work *king*. "And the woman is his mother, Queen Margaret." My face must have revealed my shock. "You broke the curse when you killed Queen Kathelina. You are a hero, and everyone is here to honor you."

"Wow, I don't know what to say." I was flabbergasted.

"You don't have to say anything, but it's time. Let's go." As the general led me into the room, trumpets sounded, and everybody stood up and began clapping. The applause nearly drowned out the triumphant music that was playing. We walked down the aisle side by side. King Hugh was smiling and clapping as was his mother. As we approached the altar, I looked to the king's right. Applauding vigorously and smiling proudly were Mitchell and Martha. I looked at Mitchell, grinned, and motioned toward Martha by raising my eyebrows. Mitchell blushed and shrugged his shoulders, smiling from ear to ear.

We stopped in front of the steps, and the queen came down to greet me. She gave me a hug and whispered, "Thank you," in my ear. King Hugh hugged me next, and then Mitchell and Martha followed. Queen Margaret then motioned for me to turn around and face the people. King Hugh stood next to me on my left with General Bernard next to the king. On my right was Mitchell, and next to him stood his lovely wife. We all faced the giant crowd that filled the church. Queen Margaret, standing behind me, put her hands on my shoulders. The clapping subsided, and the music stopped.

"Ladies and gentlemen, I give you Daniel McGunny, the savior of Annabellia."

The End

About the Author

Sean O'Neill is a full-time firefighter and paramedic for the City of Wickliffe, Ohio. Sean was raised in Lyndhurst, Ohio, and graduated from Cleveland's St. Joseph High School. He attended Kent State University from 1987 to 1991. After a twenty-six-year hiatus, Sean returned to and graduated from Kent State with a bachelor of arts and sciences in English.

Sean enjoys exercise and is an accomplished triathlete and runner and has completed a full-length Ironman Triathlon and multiple half Ironman races. Sean resides in Mentor, Ohio, with his wife, Diane; has four children; and is the loving pops to two wonderful grandchildren and the owner of a beagle named Dakota. In his free time, Sean enjoys watching sports, fishing, and spending time with his family. Sean is getting ready to retire and hopes to live on a lake and enjoy the laid-back lake life while continuing to write. *Annabellia* is Sean's first novel and will be a treasure for his family.